W9-CDI-839
WITHDRAWN

Scary Stories

ILLUSTRATED BY

BARRY MOSER

Introduction by Peter Glassman

chronicle books · san francisco

Bethlehem Central Middle School
Library Media Center

For my friend Helen Casey Brazeau —B. M.

For Jonathan, Carlie, Gabrielle, and Madeline,
my favorite little ghouls —P. G.

Illustrations © 2006 by Barry Moser.
Introduction © 2006 by Peter Glassman.
All rights reserved.

Book design by Barry Moser.
Cover design by Donna Linden.
Typeset in Bell MT, Hoefler Ornaments, and Zapf Dingbats.
Typesetting by Donna Linden.
The illustrations in this book were created with engraved blocks that were inked and printed on paper.
Manufactured in China.

Library of Congress Cataloging-in-Publication Data
Scary stories / illustrated by Barry Moser; introduction by Peter Glassman.
v. cm.
Contents: Kittens / Dean Koontz — The magic shop / H.G. Wells — Miriam / Truman Capote—The tell-tale heart / Edgar Allan Poe — Genesis and catastrophe / Roald Dahl — The squaw / Bram Stoker — Here there be tygers / Stephen King — Man overboard! / Winston Churchill — The lottery / Shirley Jackson — The bus-conductor / E. F. Benson — Thanksgiving / Joyce Carol Oates — Excerpt from The legend of Sleepy Hollow / Washington Irving — The terrible old man / H. P. Lovecraft — John Charrington's wedding / E. Nesbit — The furnished room / O. Henry — The man upstairs / Ray Bradbury — The music on the hill / Saki — The boarded window / Ambrose Bierce — Fingers on the back of the neck / Margaret Mahy — The cremation of Sam McGee / Robert Service.
ISBN-13: 978-0-8118-5414-6
ISBN-10: 0-8118-5414-0
1. Horror stories, American. 2. Horror stories, English. [1. Horror stories. 2. Short stories.] I. Moser, Barry, ill.
PZ5.S3256 2006
813'.0873808—dc22
2005025226

Distributed in Canada by Raincoast Books
9050 Shaughnessy Street, Vancouver, British Columbia V6P 6E5

10 9 8 7 6 5 4 3 2

Chronicle Books LLC
85 Second Street, San Francisco, California 94105

www.chroniclekids.com

Contents

Introduction

By Peter Glassman

A TINGLE DOWN YOUR SPINE . . . the small hairs at the back of your neck rising . . . goose bumps along your arms . . .

These are the signs of a truly scary story.

Fear is one of the most primal emotions. Like most animals, human beings are equipped with a keen sense of fear to protect us from danger and predators. With our highly developed sense of curiosity and imagination, human beings are particularly susceptible to fear of the unknown. This is why our greatest fears are often sparked by the unseen: a scratch at the window in the dark, a cry ringing out from the shadows, things that go bump in the night. . . .

Yet, oddly enough—and unlike our four-footed cousins—most people find a perverse pleasure in being scared or by being kept in suspense and anxiety over a story's outcome. Perhaps we find some satisfaction in facing our fears and standing up to them. Or perhaps it is a cathartic experience for us to survive—if only secondhand—the things that haunt our nightmares.

One thing is for certain, since people first started telling stories around a roaring fire, we have told stories of suspense and terror. And the popularity of frightening stories has never waned. Every culture around the world has myths and legends filled with cautionary warnings about the dangers of tempting the fates or trying to outwit destiny, about the terrible doings of ghosts and other terrifying creatures, and about the dire consequences of tampering in forbidden magic.

In the fourteenth century, almost two centuries before the invention of the printing press, Italian author Dante Alighieri titillated readers with his descriptions of the torments of hell with his *Inferno.* The stages of sixteenth-century England were filled with plays featuring terrifying and supernatural acts and creatures—including Shakespeare's *Macbeth* and *Hamlet.* In 1776, the very year the United States declared its independence from Britain, a Japanese scholar named Uneda Akinari published a collection of stories drawn from myths that includes a number of horrifying tales.

Tales of horror and fright truly come into their own in the nineteenth century with the publication of *Frankenstein* by Mary Shelley (Britain, 1818), *The Legend of Sleepy Hollow* by Washington Irving (United States, 1820), *The Hunchback of Notre Dame* by Victor Hugo (France, 1831), and *Nursery and Household Tales* (Kinder und Hausmarchen) by Jakob and Wilhelm Grimm (Germany, 1832). Originally, the Grimm brothers wrote their stories for adults, and included such scary fare as a "Cinderella" in which her wicked stepsisters' eyes are pecked out by doves and a "Snow White" in which the evil queen is punished by being made to dance in red-hot iron shoes; only later were these adapted for children. Then, of course, there are the many classic tales of terror written from 1833 to 1849 by American author Edgar Allan Poe, whom many deem to be the father of the modern horror story.

In the late nineteenth and early twentieth centuries, horror became a favored genre, and many of the stories from this era are still considered classics, including *The Strange Case of Dr. Jekyll and Mr. Hyde* by Robert Louis Stevenson, *The Island of Dr. Moreau* by H. G. Wells, *Dracula* by Bram Stoker, *The Picture of Dorian Gray* by Oscar Wilde, *The Monkey's Paw* by W. W. Jacobs, *Ghost Stories of an Antiquary* by M. R. James, and *The Rats in the Walls* by H. P. Lovecraft. Even authors who earned acclaim primarily as writers of children's stories or tales of drama and adventure also wrote some wonderful scary stories that were published in various magazines and newspapers of the day. Among these were Louisa May Alcott, E. Nesbit, Rudyard Kipling, O. Henry, Sir Arthur Conan Doyle, Henry James, and Charles Dickens.

Today, authors and their readers continue to be entranced by stories that arouse and excite our sense of fear. From Truman Capote to Stephen King, from Roald Dahl to Joyce Carol Oates to Ray Bradbury, few authors seem able to resist the urge to conjure up a good scare—nor do they lack for readers willing and eager to be frightened.

In this collection, we have brought together twenty very different authors—some renowned for their tales of terror and the supernatural, others best known for writing in other genres. Some are classics that have titillated and thrilled millions of readers around the world, while others are little-known gems that only devotees of horror and ghost stories are likely to have come across before.

Few in America can get through high school without encountering Edgar Allan Poe's gruesome short story "The Tell-Tale Heart" or Washington Irving's at turns comical and horrific *The Legend of Sleepy Hollow*. But did you know that Britain's great prime minister Sir Winston Churchill penned a chilling tale called "Man Overboard!"? Or that O. Henry, famous for such hilarious and ironic short stories as "The Ransom of Red Chief" and "The Gift of the Magi," could create a tale as haunting as "The Furnished Room"?

Roald Dahl is familiar to most as the author of *Charlie and the Chocolate Factory*, but he's also a master of the macabre, as "Genesis and Catastrophe" attests. Who doesn't know Stephen King? He's the famous best-selling author of numerous modern classics of horror, such as *Salem's Lot*, *The Shining*, and *It*. Though his terrifying novels are the most well known, he is also a brilliant short story writer, as you'll learn in "Here There Be Tygers."

When you hear the name H. G. Wells, his classics of science fiction *War of the Worlds* and *The Time Machine* leap to mind, while mention Ray Bradbury and one automatically thinks of *The Martian Chronicles* and *Fahrenheit 451*. But the fear and tension in those books is nothing compared to the chills you'll find in Wells's "The Magic Shop" and Bradbury's "The Man Upstairs."

E. Nesbit was a beloved children's writer. Among her endearing stories of adventure and magic are *The Railway Children* and *The Story of the*

Treasure Seekers, yet she also had a darker side, which is on display in her eerie story "John Charrington's Wedding." Truman Capote rose to international fame with *In Cold Blood* and *Breakfast at Tiffany's*, but he penned a marvelously eerie and creepy tale in "Miriam."

As we contemplated an illustrator for this collection, we naturally thought of Barry Moser. His haunting and brilliant engravings for *Frankenstein* (1984) and his spine-tingling watercolors for *Tales of Edgar Allan Poe* (1991) are among the most striking and memorable illustrations ever created for these classic works of horror. Moser's genius lies in his ability to capture a story in a single moment, bringing it vividly to life, and so convey the emotional impact of the author's words through his art. In the twenty heart-stopping, eerie, and mesmerizing engravings he has created for this book, Moser has crafted a suite of images that portrays the range of moods, settings, and emotions that reflect the diversity of the wonderful talents collected here.

From the poignant picture in the cemetery for "John Charrington's Wedding" to the horrifying image of the hand dripping blood for "Kittens"; from the searing eyes that stare out from the young girl's face in the picture for "Miriam" to the harrowing visage of the Headless Horseman for *The Legend of Sleepy Hollow*; from the creepy image of the knife held over the victim in "The Tell-Tale Heart" to the terrifying view of the attacking cat—claws fully extended—for "The Squaw": Moser flawlessly captures the frights that spring from these fabulous authors' words.

So steel your nerves, steady your pulse, curl up someplace brightly lit (or, if you're truly brave, read these pages by a candle's flickering light), and prepare to be scared as you've rarely been scared before by entering into the brilliantly horrifying worlds of these twenty great tales of terror.

Kittens

By Dean Koontz

The cool green water slipped along the streambed, bubbling around smooth brown stones, reflecting the melancholy willows that lined the bank. Marnie sat on the grass, tossing stones into a deep pool, watching the ripples spread in ever-widening circles and lap at the muddy banks. She was thinking about the kittens. This year's kittens, not last year's. A year ago, her parents had told her that the kittens had gone to Heaven. Pinkie's litter had disappeared the third day after their squealing birth.

Marnie's father had said, "God took them away to Heaven to live with Him."

She didn't exactly doubt her father. After all, he was a religious man. He taught Sunday school every week and was an officer or something in the church, whose duty it was to count collection money and mark it down in a little red book. He was always picked to give the sermon on Laymen's Sunday. And every evening, he read passages to them from the Bible. She had been late for the reading last night and had been spanked. "Spare the rod and spoil the child," her father always said. No, she didn't actually doubt her father, for if anyone would know about God and kittens, it was he.

But she continued to wonder. Why, when there were hundreds upon thousands of kittens in the world, did God have to take all four of hers? Was God selfish?

This was the first that she had thought of those kittens for some time. In the past twelve months, much had happened to make her forget. There was her first year in school, the furor of getting ready for the first day—

the buying of paper, pencils, and books. And the first few weeks had been interesting, meeting Mr. Alphabet and Mr. Numbers. When school began to bore her, Christmas rushed in on polished runners and glistening ice: the shopping, the green and yellow and red and blue lights, the Santa Claus on the corner who staggered when he walked, the candlelit church on Christmas Eve when she had had to go to the bathroom and her father had made her wait until the service was over. When things began to lose momentum again in March, her mother had given birth to twins. Marnie had been surprised at how small they were and at how slowly they seemed to grow in the following weeks.

Here it was June again. The twins were three months old, finally beginning to grow a great deal heavier; school was out, and Christmas was an eternity away, and everything was getting dull again. Therefore, when she heard her father telling her mother that Pinkie was going to have another litter, she grasped at the news and wrenched every drop of excitement from it. She busied herself in the kitchen, preparing rags and cotton for the birth and a fancy box for the kittens' home when they arrived.

As events ran their natural course, Pinkie slunk away and had the kittens during the night in a dark corner of the barn. There was no need for sterilized rags or cotton, but the box came in handy. There were six in this litter, all gray with black spots that looked like ink hastily blotted.

She liked the kittens, and she was worried about them. What if God was watching again like last year?

"What are you doing, Marnie?"

She didn't have to look; she knew who was behind her. She turned anyway, out of deference, and saw her father glaring down at her, dark irregular splotches of perspiration discoloring the underarms of his faded blue work coveralls, dirt smeared on his chin and caked to the beard on his left cheek.

"Throwing stones," she answered quietly.

"At the fish?"

"Oh, no, sir. Just throwing stones."

"Do we remember who was the victim of stone throwing?" He smiled a patronizing smile.

"Saint Stephen," she answered.

"Very good." The smile faded. "Supper's ready."

She sat ramrod stiff in the old maroon easy chair, looking attentive as her father read to them from the ancient family Bible that was bound in black leather, all scuffed and with several torn pages. Her mother sat next to her father on the dark blue corduroy couch, hands folded in her lap, an isn't-it-wonderful-what-God-has-given-us smile painted on her plain but pretty face.

"Suffer the little children to come to me, and forbid them not; for such is the kingdom of God." Her father closed the book with a gentle slap that seemed to leap into the stale air and hang there, holding up a thick curtain of silence. No one spoke for several minutes. Then: "What chapter of what book did we just read, Marnie?"

"Saint Mark, chapter ten," she said dutifully.

"Fine," he said. Turning to his wife, whose smile had changed to a we've-done-what-a-Christian-family-should-do expression, he said, "Mary, how about coffee for us and a glass of milk for Marnie?"

"Right," said her mother, getting up and pacing into the kitchen.

Her father sat there, examining the inside covers of the old holy book, running his fingers along the cracks in the yellow paper, scrutinizing the ghostly stains embedded forever in the title page where some great-uncle had accidentally spilled wine a million-billion years ago.

"Father," she said tentatively.

He looked up from the book, not smiling, not frowning.

"What about the kittens?"

"What about them?" he countered.

"Will God take them again this year?"

The half-smile that had crept onto his face evaporated into the thick air of the living room. "Perhaps," was all that he said.

"He can't," she almost sobbed.

"Are you saying what God can and cannot do, young lady?"

"No, sir."

"God can do anything."

"Yes, sir." She fidgeted in her chair, pushing herself deeper into its rough, worn folds. "But why would he want my kittens again? Why always mine?"

"I've had quite enough of this, Marnie. Now be quiet."

"Buy why mine?" she persisted.

He stood suddenly, crossed to the chair, and slapped her delicate face. A thin trickle of blood slipped from the corner of her mouth. She wiped it away with the palm of her hand.

"You must not doubt God's motives!" her father insisted. "You are far too young to doubt." The saliva glistened on his lips. He grabbed her by the arm and brought her to her feet. "Now you get up those stairs and into bed."

She didn't argue. On the way to the staircase, she wiped away the re-forming stream of blood. She walked slowly up the steps, allowing her hand to run along the smooth, polished wood railing.

"Here's the milk," she heard her mother saying below.

"We won't be needing it," her father answered curtly.

In her room, she lay in the semidarkness that came when the full moon shone through her window, its orange-yellow light glinting from a row of religious plaques that lined one wall. In her parents' room, her mother was cooing to the twins, changing their diapers. "God's little angels," she heard her mother say. Her father was tickling them, and she could hear the "angels" chuckling—a deep gurgle that rippled from down in their fat throats.

Neither her father nor her mother came to say good night. She was being punished.

Marnie was sitting in the barn, petting one of the gray kittens, postponing an errand her mother had sent her on ten minutes earlier. The rich smell of dry, golden hay filled the air. Straw covered the floor and crackled underfoot. In the far end of the building, the cows were lowing to each other—only two of them, whose legs had been sliced by barbed wire and who were being made to convalesce. The kitten mewed and pawed the air below her chin.

"Where's Marnie?" her father's voice boomed from somewhere in the yard between the house and the barn.

She was about to answer when she heard her mother call from the house: "I sent her to Brown's for a recipe of Helen's. She'll be gone another twenty minutes."

"That's plenty of time," her father answered. The crunch of his heavy shoes on the cinder path echoed in military rhythm.

Marnie knew that something was wrong; something was happening that she was not supposed to see. Quickly, she put the kitten back in the red and gold box and sprawled behind a pile of straw to watch.

Her father entered, drew a bucket of water from the wall tap, and placed it in front of the kittens. Pinkie hissed and arched her back. The man picked her up and shut her in an empty oat bin from which her anguished squeals boomed in a ridiculously loud echo that belonged on the African veldt and not on an American farm. Marnie almost laughed, but remembered her father and suppressed the levity.

He turned again to the box of kittens. Carefully, he lifted one by the scruff of the neck, petted it twice, and thrust its head under the water in the bucket! There was a violent thrashing from within the bucket, and sparkling droplets of water sprayed into the air. Her father grimaced and shoved the entire body under the smothering pool. In time, the thrashing ceased. Marnie found that her fingers were digging into the concrete floor, hurting her.

Why? Why-why-why?

Her father lifted the limp body from the bucket. Something pink and bloody hung from the animal's mouth. She couldn't tell whether it was the tongue or whether the precious thing had spewed its entrails into the water in a last attempt to escape the heavy, horrible death of suffocation.

Soon six kittens were dead. Soon six silent fur balls were dropped in a burlap sack. The top was twisted shut. He let Pinkie out of the bin. The shivering cat followed him out of the barn, mewing softly, hissing when he turned to look at her.

Marnie lay very still for a long time, thinking of nothing but the execution and trying desperately to understand. Had God sent her father? Was it God who told him to kill the kittens—to take them away from her? If it was,

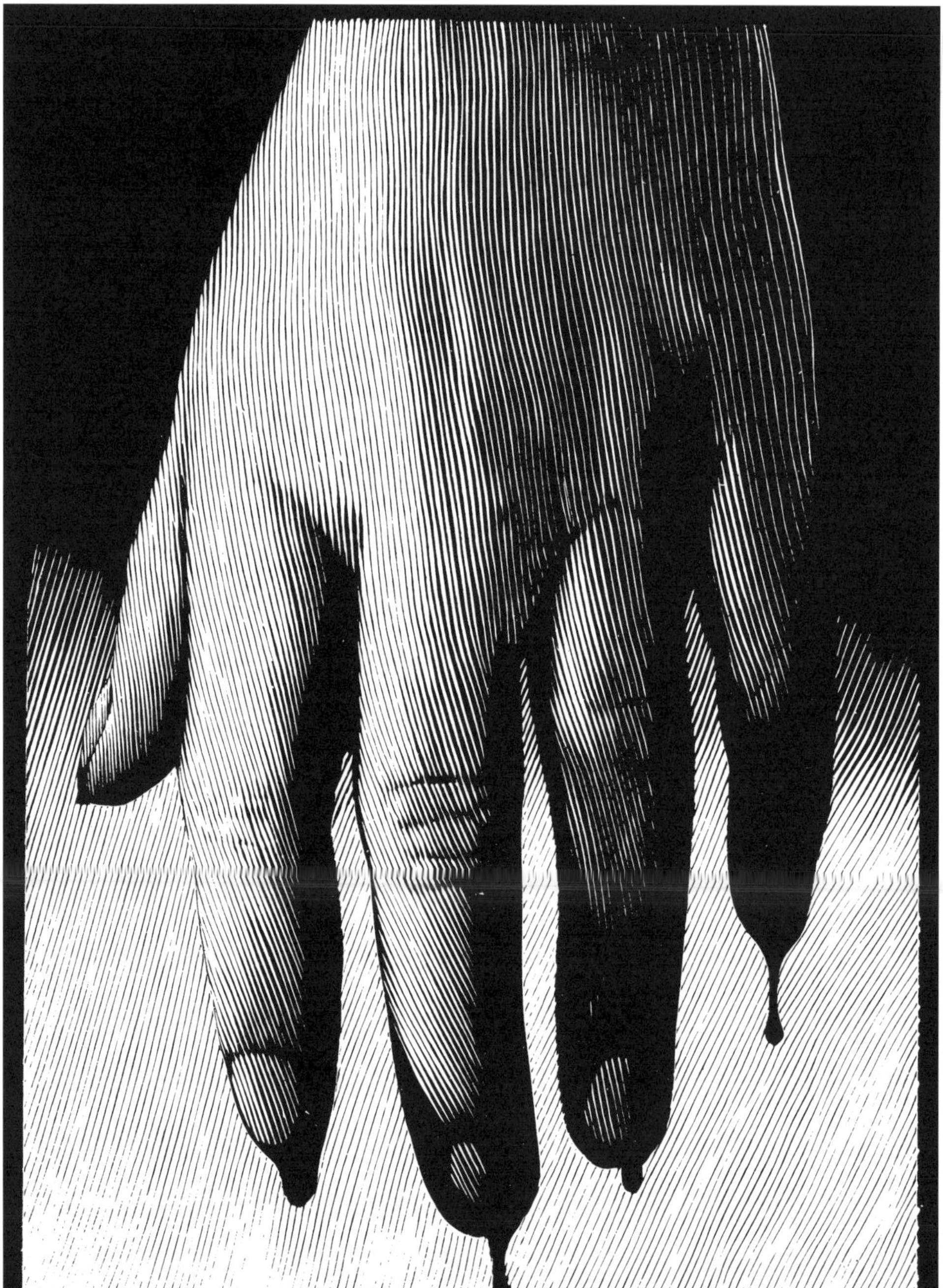

Blood dripping from her fingers.

she didn't see how she could ever again stand before that gold and white altar, accepting communion. She stood and walked toward the house, blood dripping from her fingers, blood and cement.

"Did you get the recipe?" asked her mother as Marnie slammed the kitchen door.

"Mrs. Brown couldn't find it. She'll send it over tomorrow." She lied so well that she surprised herself. "Did God take my kittens?" she blurted suddenly.

Her mother looked confused. "Yes," was all that she could say.

"I'll get even with God! He can't do that! He can't!" She ran out of the kitchen toward the staircase.

Her mother watched but didn't try to stop her.

Marnie Caufield walked slowly up the stairs, letting her hand run along the smooth, polished wood railing.

At noon, when Walter Caufield came in from the field, he heard a loud crash and the tinkling of china and the shattering of glass. He rushed into the living room to see his wife lying at the foot of the stairs. A novelty table was overturned, statuettes broken and cracked.

"Mary, Mary. Are you hurt?" He bent quickly to her side.

She looked up at him out of eyes that were far away in distant mists. "Walt! My Good God, Walt—our precious angels. The bathtub—our precious angels!"

The Magic Shop

By H. G. Wells

I HAD SEEN the Magic Shop from afar several times; I had passed it once or twice, a shop window of alluring little objects, magic balls, magic hens, wonderful cones, ventriloquist dolls, the material of the basket trick, packs of cards that *looked* all right, and all that sort of thing, but never had I thought of going in until one day, almost without warning, Gip hauled me by my finger right up to the window, and so conducted himself that there was nothing for it but to take him in. I had not thought the place was there, to tell the truth—a modest-sized frontage in Regent Street, between the picture shop and the place where the chicks run about just out of patent incubators—but there it was sure enough. I had fancied it was down nearer the Circus, or round the corner in Oxford Street, or even in Holborn; always over the way and a little inaccessible it had been, with something of the mirage in its position; but here it was now quite indisputably, and the fat end of Gip's pointing finger made a noise upon the glass.

"If I was rich," said Gip, dabbing a finger at the Disappearing Egg, "I'd buy myself that. And that"—which was The Crying Baby, Very Human—"and that," which was a mystery, and called, so a neat card asserted, "Buy One and Astonish Your Friends."

"Anything," said Gip, "will disappear under one of those cones. I have read about it in a book.

"And there, dadda, is the Vanishing Halfpenny—only they've put it this way up so's we can't see how it's done."

Gip, dear boy, inherits his mother's breeding, and he did not propose to enter the shop or worry in any way; only, you know, quite unconsciously he lugged my finger doorward, and he made his interest clear.

"That," he said, and pointed to the Magic Bottle.

"If you had that?" I said; at which promising inquiry he looked up with a sudden radiance.

"I could show it to Jessie," he said, thoughtful as ever of others.

"It's less than a hundred days to your birthday, Gibbles," I said, and laid my hand on the door-handle.

Gip made no answer, but his grip tightened on my finger, and so we came into the shop.

It was no common shop this; it was a magic shop, and all the prancing precedence Gip would have taken in the matter of mere toys was wanting. He left the burden of the conversation to me.

It was a little, narrow shop, not very well lit, and the door-bell pinged again with a plaintive note as we closed it behind us. For a moment or so we were alone and could glance about us. There was a tiger in *papier-mâché* on the glass case that covered the low counter—a grave, kind-eyed tiger that waggled his head in a methodical manner; there were several crystal spheres, a china hand holding magic cards, a stock of magic fish-bowls in various sizes, and an immodest magic hat that shamelessly displayed its springs. On the floor were magic mirrors; one to draw you out long and thin, one to swell your head and vanish your legs, and one to make you short and fat like a draught; and while we were laughing at these the shopman, as I suppose, came in.

At any rate, there he was behind the counter—a curious, sallow, dark man, with one ear larger than the other and a chin like the toe-cap of a boot.

"What can we have the pleasure?" he said, spreading his long, magic fingers on the glass case; and so with a start we were aware of him.

"I want," I said, "to buy my little boy a few simple tricks."

"Legerdemain?" he asked. "Mechanical? Domestic?"

"Anything amusing?" said I.

"Um!" said the shopman, and scratched his head for a moment as if thinking. Then, quite distinctly, he drew from his head a glass ball. "Something in this way?" he said, and held it out.

The action was unexpected. I had seen the trick done at entertainments endless times before—it's part of the common stock of conjurers—but I had not expected it here. "That's good," I said, with a laugh.

"Isn't it?" said the shopman.

Gip stretched out his disengaged hand to take this object and found merely a blank palm.

"It's in your pocket," said the shopman, and there it was!

"How much will that be?" I asked.

"We make no charge for glass balls," said the shopman, politely. "We get them"—he picked one out of his elbow as he spoke—"free." He produced another from the back of his neck, and laid it beside its predecessor on the counter. Gip regarded his glass ball sagely, then directed a look of inquiry at the two on the counter, and finally brought his round-eyed scrutiny to the shopman, who smiled. "You may have those too," said the shopman, "and, if you *don't* mind, one from my mouth—*So!*"

Gip counseled me mutely for a moment, and then in a profound silence put away the four balls, resumed my reassuring finger, and nerved himself for the next event.

"We get all our smaller tricks in that way," the shopman remarked.

I laughed in the manner of one who subscribes to a jest. "Instead of going to the wholesale shop," I said. "Of course, it's cheaper."

"In a way," the shopman said. "Though we pay in the end. But not so heavily—as people suppose. . . . Our larger tricks, and our daily provisions and all the other things we want, we get out of that hat. And you know, sir, if you'll excuse my saying it, there *isn't* a wholesale shop, not for Genuine Magic goods, sir. I don't know if you noticed our inscription—the Genuine Magic shop." He drew a business card from his cheek and handed it to me. "Genuine," he said, with his finger on the word, and added, "There is absolutely no deception, sir."

He seemed to be carrying out the joke pretty thoroughly, I thought.

He turned to Gip with a smile of remarkable affability. "You, you know, are the Right Sort of Boy."

I was surprised at his knowing that, because, in the interests of discipline, we keep it rather a secret even at home; but Gip received it in unflinching silence, keeping a steadfast eye on him.

"It's only the Right Sort of Boy gets through that doorway."

And, as if by way of illustration, there came a rattling at the door, and a squeaking little voice could be faintly heard. "Nyar! I *warn* 'a go in there, dadda, I WARN 'a go in there. Nya-a-a-ah!" and then the accents of a down-trodden parent, urging consolations and propitiations. "It's locked, Edward," he said.

"But it isn't," said I.

"It is, sir," said the shopman, "always—for that sort of child," and as he spoke we had a glimpse of the other youngster, a small white face, pallid from sweet-eating and over-sapid food, and distorted by evil passions, a ruthless little egotist, pawing at the enchanted pane. "It's no good, sir," said the shopman, as I moved, with my natural helpfulness, doorward, and presently the spoiled child was carried off howling.

"How do you manage that?" I said, breathing a little more freely.

"Magic!" said the shopman, with a careless wave of the hand, and behold! sparks of colored fire flew out of his fingers and vanished into the shadows of the shop.

"You were saying," he said, addressing himself to Gip, "before you came in, that you would like one of our 'Buy One and Astonish Your Friends' boxes?"

Gip, after a gallant effort, said "Yes."

"It's in your pocket."

And leaning over the counter—he really had an extraordinarily long body—this amazing person produced the article in the customary conjurer's manner. "Paper," he said, and took a sheet out of the empty hat with the springs; "string," and behold his mouth was a string-box, from which he drew an unending thread, which when he had tied his parcel he bit off—and, it seemed to me, swallowed the ball of string. And then he lit a candle at the nose of one of the ventriloquist's dummies, stuck one of his fingers (which had become sealing-wax red) into the flame, and so sealed the parcel. "Then there was the Disappearing Egg," he remarked, and produced one from within my coat-breast and packed it, and also The Crying Baby, Very Human. I handed each parcel to Gip as it was ready, and he clasped them to his chest.

He said very little, but his eyes were eloquent; the clutch of his arms was eloquent. He was the playground of unspeakable emotions. These, you know, were *real* Magics.

Then, with a start, I discovered something moving about in my hat—something soft and jumpy. I whipped it off, and a ruffled pigeon—no doubt a confederate—dropped out and ran on the counter, and went, I fancy, into a cardboard box behind the *papier-mâché* tiger.

"Tut, tut!" said the shopman, dexterously relieving me of my headdress; "careless bird, and—as I live—nesting!"

He shook my hat, and shook out into his extended hand two or three eggs, a large marble, a watch, about half-a-dozen of the inevitable glass balls, and then crumpled, crinkled paper, more and more and more, talking all the time of the way in which people neglect to brush their hats *inside* as well as out, politely, of course, but with a certain personal application. "All sorts of things accumulate, sir. . . . Not *you*, of course, in particular. . . . Nearly every customer. . . . Astonishing what they carry about with them. . . ." The crumpled paper rose and billowed on the counter more and more and more, until he was nearly hidden from us, until he was altogether hidden, and still his voice went on and on. "We none of us know what the fair semblance of a human being may conceal, sir. Are we all then no better than brushed exteriors, whited sepulchres—"

His voice stopped—exactly like when you hit a neighbor's gramophone with a well-aimed brick, the same instant silence, and the rustle of the paper stopped, and everything was still. . . .

"Have you done with my hat?" I said, after an interval.

There was no answer

I stared at Gip, and Gip stared at me, and there were our distortions in the magic mirrors, looking very rum, and grave, and quiet. . . .

"I think we'll go now," I said. "Will you tell me how much all this comes to? . . .

"I say," I said, on a rather louder note, "I want the bill; and my hat, please."

It might have been a sniff from behind the paper pile. . . .

"Let's look behind the counter, Gip," I said. "He's making fun of us."

I led Gip round the head-wagging tiger, and what do you think there was behind the counter? No one at all! Only my hat on the floor, and a common conjurer's lop-eared white rabbit lost in meditation, and looking as stupid and crumpled as only a conjurer's rabbit can do. I resumed my hat, and the rabbit lolloped a lollop or so out of my way.

There were our distortions in the magic mirrors.

"Dadda!" said Gip, in a guilty whisper.

"What is it, Gip?" said I.

"I *do* like this shop, dadda."

"So should I," I said to myself, "if the counter wouldn't suddenly extend itself to shut one off from the door." But I didn't call Gip's attention to that. "Pussy!" he said, with a hand out to the rabbit as it came lolloping past us; "Pussy, do Gip a magic!" and his eyes followed it as it squeezed through a door I had certainly not remarked a moment before. Then this door opened wider, and the man with one ear larger than the other appeared again. He was smiling still, but his eye met mine with something between amusement and defiance. "You'd like to see our showroom, sir," he said, with an innocent suavity. Gip tugged my finger forward. I glanced at the counter and met the shopman's eye again. I was beginning to think the magic just a little too genuine. "We haven't *very* much time," I said. But somehow we were inside the showroom before I could finish that.

"All goods of the same quality," said the shopman, rubbing his flexible hands together, "and that is the Best. Nothing in the place that isn't genuine Magic, and warranted thoroughly rum. Excuse me, sir!"

I felt him pull at something that clung to my coat-sleeve, and then I saw he held a little, wriggling red demon by the tail—the little creature bit and fought and tried to get at his hand—and in a moment he tossed it carelessly behind a counter. No doubt the thing was only an image of twisted India rubber, but for the moment—! And his gesture was exactly that of a man who handles some petty biting bit of vermin. I glanced at Gip, but Gip was looking at a magic rocking horse. I was glad he hadn't seen the thing. "I say," I said, in an undertone, and indicating Gip and the red demon with my eyes, "you haven't many things like *that* about, have you?"

"None of ours! Probably brought it with you," said the shopman—also in an undertone, and with a more dazzling smile than ever. "Astonishing what people *will* carry about with them unawares!" And then to Gip, "Do you see anything you fancy here?"

There were many things that Gip fancied there.

He turned to this astonishing tradesman with mingled confidence and respect. "Is that a Magic Sword?" he said.

"A Magic Toy Sword. It neither bends, breaks, nor cuts the fingers. It renders the bearer invincible in battle against anyone under eighteen. Half-a-crown to seven and sixpence, according to size. These panoplies on cards are for juvenile knights-errant and very useful—shield of safety, sandals of swiftness, helmet of invisibility."

"Oh, daddy!" gasped Gip.

I tried to find out what they cost, but the shopman did not heed me. He had got Gip now; he had got him away from my finger; he had embarked upon the exposition of all his confounded stock, and nothing was going to stop him. Presently I saw with a qualm of distrust and something very like jealousy that Gip had hold of this person's finger as usually he has hold of mine. No doubt the fellow was interesting, I thought, and had an interestingly faked lot of stuff, really *good* faked stuff, still—

I wandered after them, saying very little, but keeping an eye on this prestidigital fellow. After all, Gip was enjoying it. And no doubt when the time came to go we should be able to go quite easily.

It was a long, rambling place, that showroom, a gallery broken up by stands and stalls and pillars, with archways leading off to other departments, in which the queerest-looking assistants loafed and stared at one, and with perplexing mirrors and curtains. So perplexing, indeed, were these that I was presently unable to make out the door by which we had come.

The shopman showed Gip magic trains that ran without steam or clockwork, just as you set the signals, and then some very, very valuable boxes of soldiers that all came alive directly you took off the lid and said—I myself haven't a very quick ear and it was a tongue-twisting sound, but Gip—he has his mother's ear—got it in no time. "Bravo!" said the shopman, putting the men back into the box unceremoniously and handing it to Gip. "Now," said the shopman, and in a moment Gip had made them all alive again.

"You'll take that box?" asked the shopman.

"We'll take that box," said I, "unless you charge its full value. In which case it would need a Trust Magnate—"

"Dear heart! *No!*" and the shopman swept the little men back again, shut the lid, waved the box in the air, and there it was, in brown paper, tied up and—*with Gip's full name and address on the paper!*

The shopman laughed at my amazement.

"This is the genuine Magic," he said. "The real thing."

"It's a little too genuine for my taste," I said again.

After that he fell to showing Gip tricks, odd tricks, and still odder the way they were done. He explained them, he turned them inside out, and there was the dear little chap nodding his busy bit of a head in the sagest manner.

I did not attend as well as I might. "Hey, presto!" said the Magic Shopman, and then would come the clear, small "Hey, presto!" of the boy. But I was distracted by other things. It was being borne in upon me just how tremendously rum this place was; it was, so to speak, inundated by a sense of rumness. There was something vaguely rum about the fixtures even, about the ceiling, about the floor, about the casually distributed chairs. I had a queer feeling that whenever I wasn't looking at them straight they went askew, and moved about, and played a noiseless puss-in-the-corner behind my back. And the cornice had a serpentine design with masks—masks altogether too expressive for proper plaster.

Then abruptly my attention was caught by one of the odd-looking assistants. He was some way off and evidently unaware of my presence—I saw a sort of three-quarter length of him over a pile of toys and through an arch—and, you know, he was leaning against a pillar in an idle sort of way doing the most horrid things with his features! The particular horrid thing he did was with his nose. He did it just as though he was idle and wanted to amuse himself. First of all it was a short, blobby nose, and then suddenly he shot it out like a telescope, and then out it flew and became thinner and thinner until it was like a long, red, flexible whip. Like a thing in a nightmare it was! He flourished it about and flung it forth as a fly fisher flings his line

My instant thought was that Gip mustn't see him. I turned about, and there was Gip quite preoccupied with the shopman, and thinking no evil. They were whispering together and looking at me. Gip was standing on a stool, and the shopman was holding a sort of big drum in his hand.

"Hide and seek, dadda!" cried Gip. "You're He!"

And before I could do anything to prevent it, the shopman had clapped the big drum over him.

I saw what was up directly. "Take that off," I cried, "this instant! You'll frighten the boy. Take it off!"

The shopman with the unequal ears did so without a word, and held the big cylinder towards me to show its emptiness. And the little stool was vacant! In that instant my boy had utterly disappeared! . . .

You know, perhaps, that sinister something that comes like a hand out of the unseen and grips your heart about. You know it takes your common self away and leaves you tense and deliberate, neither slow nor hasty, neither angry nor afraid. So it was with me.

I came up to this grinning shopman and kicked his stool aside.

"Stop this folly!" I said. "Where is my boy?"

"You see," he said, still displaying the drum's interior, "there is no deception—"

I put out my hand to grip him, and he eluded me by a dexterous movement. I snatched again, and he turned from me and pushed open a door to escape. "Stop!" I said, and he laughed, receding. I leapt after him—into utter darkness.

Thud!

"Lor' bless my 'eart! I didn't see you coming, sir!"

I was in Regent Street, and I had collided with a decent-looking working man; and a yard away, perhaps, and looking extremely perplexed with himself, was Gip. There was some sort of apology, and then Gip had turned and come to me with a bright little smile, as though for a moment he had missed me.

And he was carrying four parcels in his arm!

He secured immediate possession of my finger.

For the second I was rather at a loss. I stared round to see the door of the magic shop, and, behold, it was not there! There was no door, no shop, nothing, only the common pilaster between the shop where they sell pictures and the window with the chicks! . . .

I did the only thing possible in that mental tumult; I walked straight to the curbstone and held up my umbrella for a cab.

"'Ansoms," said Gip, in a note of culminating exultation.

I helped him in, recalled my address with an effort, and got in also. Something unusual proclaimed itself in my tail-coat pocket, and I felt and discovered a glass ball. With a petulant expression I flung it into the street.

Gip said nothing.

For a space neither of us spoke.

"Dadda!" said Gip, at last, "that *was* a proper shop!"

I came round with that to the problem of just how the whole thing had seemed to him. He looked completely undamaged—so far, good; he was neither scared nor unhinged, he was simply tremendously satisfied with the afternoon's entertainment, and there in his arms were the four parcels.

Confound it! what could be in them?

"Um!" I said. "Little boys can't go to shops like that every day."

He received this with his usual stoicism, and for a moment I was sorry I was his father and not his mother, and so couldn't suddenly there, *coram publico,* in our hansom, kiss him. After all, I thought, the thing wasn't so very bad.

But it was only when we opened the parcels that I really began to be reassured. Three of them contained boxes of soldiers, quite ordinary lead soldiers, but of so good a quality as to make Gip altogether forget that originally these parcels had been Magic Tricks of the only genuine sort, and the fourth contained a kitten, a little living white kitten, in excellent health and appetite and temper.

I saw this unpacking with a sort of provisional relief. I hung about in the nursery for quite an unconscionable time. . . .

That happened six months ago. And now I am beginning to believe it is all right. The kitten had only the magic natural to all kittens, and the soldiers seem as steady a company as any colonel could desire. And Gip—?

The intelligent parent will understand that I have to go cautiously with Gip.

But I went so far as this one day. I said, "How would you like your soldiers to come alive, Gip, and march about by themselves?"

"Mine do," said Gip. "I just have to say a word I know before I open the lid."

"Then they march about alone?"

"Oh, *quite*, dadda. I shouldn't like them if they didn't do that."

I displayed no unbecoming surprise, and since then I have taken occasion to drop in upon him once or twice, unannounced, when the soldiers were about, but so far I have never discovered them performing in anything like a magical manner. . . .

It's so difficult to tell.

There's also a question of finance. I have an incurable habit of paying bills. I have been up and down Regent Street several times, looking for that shop. I am inclined to think, indeed, that in that matter honor is satisfied, and that, since Gip's name and address are known to them, I may very well leave it to these people, whoever they may be, to send in their bill in their own time.

Miriam

By Truman Capote

For several years, Mrs. H. T. Miller had lived alone in a pleasant apartment (two rooms with kitchenette) in a remodeled brownstone near the East River. She was a widow: Mr. H. T. Miller had left a reasonable amount of insurance. Her interests were narrow, she had no friends to speak of, and she rarely journeyed farther than the corner grocer. The other people in the house never seemed to notice her: her clothes were matter-of-fact, her hair iron-gray, clipped and casually waved; she did not use cosmetics, her features were plain and inconspicuous, and on her last birthday she was sixty-one. Her activities were seldom spontaneous: she kept the two rooms immaculate, smoked an occasional cigarette, prepared her own meals, and tended a canary.

Then she met Miriam. It was snowing that night. Mrs. Miller had finished drying the supper dishes and was thumbing through an afternoon paper when she saw an advertisement of a picture playing at a neighborhood theater. The title sounded good, so she struggled into her beaver coat, laced her galoshes, and left the apartment, leaving one light burning in the foyer: she found nothing more disturbing than a sensation of darkness.

The snow was fine, falling gently, not yet making an impression on the pavement. The wind from the river cut only at street crossings. Mrs. Miller hurried, her head bowed, oblivious as a mole burrowing a blind path. She stopped at a drugstore and bought a package of peppermints.

A long line stretched in front of the box office; she took her place at the end. There would be (a tired voice groaned) a short wait for all seats. Mrs.

Miller rummaged in her leather handbag till she collected exactly the correct change for admission. The line seemed to be taking its own time and, looking around for some distraction, she suddenly became conscious of a little girl standing under the edge of the marquee.

Her hair was the longest and strangest Mrs. Miller had ever seen: absolutely silver-white, like an albino's. It flowed waist-length in smooth, loose lines. She was thin and fragilely constructed. There was a simple, special elegance in the way she stood with her thumbs in the pockets of a tailored plum-velvet coat.

Mrs. Miller felt oddly excited, and when the little girl glanced toward her, she smiled warmly. The little girl walked over and said, "Would you care to do me a favor?"

"I'd be glad to, if I can," said Mrs. Miller.

"Oh, it's quite easy. I merely want you to buy a ticket for me; they won't let me in otherwise. Here, I have the money." And gracefully she handed Mrs. Miller two dimes and a nickel.

They went over to the theater together. An usherette directed them to a lounge; in twenty minutes the picture would be over.

"I feel just like a genuine criminal," said Mrs. Miller gaily, as she sat down. "I mean, that sort of thing's against the law, isn't it? I do hope I haven't done the wrong thing. Your mother knows where you are, dear? I mean she does, doesn't she?"

The little girl said nothing. She unbuttoned her coat and folded it across her lap. Her dress underneath was prim and dark blue. A gold chain dangled about her neck, and her fingers, sensitive and musical-looking, toyed with it. Examining her more attentively, Mrs. Miller decided the truly distinctive feature was not her hair, but her eyes; they were hazed, steady, lacking any childlike quality whatsoever and, because of their size, seemed to consume her small face.

Mrs. Miller offered a peppermint. "What's your name, dear?"

"Miriam," she said, as though, in some curious way, it were information already familiar.

"Why, isn't that funny—my name's Miriam, too. And it's not a terribly common name either. Now, don't tell me your last name's Miller!"

"Just Miriam."

"But isn't that funny?"

"Moderately," said Miriam, and rolled the peppermint on her tongue.

Mrs. Miller flushed and shifted uncomfortably. "You have such a large vocabulary for such a little girl."

"Do I?"

"Well, yes," said Mrs. Miller, hastily changing the topic to: "Do you like the movies?"

"I really wouldn't know," said Miriam. "I've never been before."

Women began filling the lounge; the rumble of the newsreel bombs exploded in the distance. Mrs. Miller rose, tucking her purse under her arm. "I guess I'd better be running now if I want to get a seat," she said. "It was nice to have met you."

Miriam nodded ever so slightly.

—

It snowed all week. Wheels and footsteps moved soundlessly on the street, as if the business of living continued secretly behind a pale but impenetrable curtain. In the falling quiet there was no sky or earth, only snow lifting in the wind, frosting the window glass, chilling the rooms, deadening and hushing the city. At all hours it was necessary to keep a lamp lighted, and Mrs. Miller lost track of the days: Friday was no different from Saturday and on Sunday she went to the grocery: closed, of course.

That evening she scrambled eggs and fixed a bowl of tomato soup. Then, after putting on a flannel robe and cold-creaming her face, she propped herself up in bed with a hot-water bottle under her feet. She was reading the *Times* when the doorbell rang. At first she thought it must be a mistake and whoever it was would go away. But it rang and rang and settled to a persistent buzz. She looked at the clock: a little after eleven; it did not seem possible, she was always asleep by ten.

Climbing out of bed, she trotted barefoot across the living room. "I'm coming, please be patient." The latch was caught; she turned it this way and that way and the bell never paused an instant. "Stop it," she cried. The bolt gave way and she opened the door an inch. "What in heaven's name?"

"Hello," said Miriam.

"Oh . . . why, hello," said Mrs. Miller, stepping hesitantly into the hall. "You're that little girl."

"I thought you'd never answer, but I kept my finger on the button; I knew you were home. Aren't you glad to see me?"

Mrs. Miller did not know what to say. Miriam, she saw, wore the same plum-velvet coat and now she had also a beret to match; her white hair was braided in two shining plaits and looped at the ends with enormous white ribbons.

"Since I've waited so long, you could at least let me in," she said.

"It's awfully late. . . ."

Miriam regarded her blankly. "What difference does that make? Let me in. It's cold out here and I have on a silk dress." Then, with a gentle gesture, she urged Mrs. Miller aside and passed into the apartment.

She dropped her coat and beret on a chair. She was indeed wearing a silk dress. White silk. White silk in February. The skirt was beautifully pleated and the sleeves long; it made a faint rustle as she strolled about the room. "I like your place," she said. "I like the rug, blue's my favorite color." She touched a paper rose in a vase on the coffee table. "Imitation," she commented wanly. "How sad. Aren't imitations sad?" She seated herself on the sofa, daintily spreading her skirt.

"What do you want?" asked Mrs. Miller.

"Sit down," said Miriam. "It makes me nervous to see people stand."

Mrs. Miller sank to a hassock. "What do you want?" she repeated.

"You know, I don't think you're glad I came."

For a second time Mrs. Miller was without an answer; her hand motioned vaguely. Miriam giggled and pressed back on a mound of chintz pillows. Mrs. Miller observed that the girl was less pale than she remembered; her cheeks were flushed.

"How did you know where I lived?"

Miriam frowned. "That's no question at all. What's your name? What's mine?"

"But I'm not listed in the phone book."

"Oh, let's talk about something else."

Mrs. Miller said, "Your mother must be insane to let a child like you wander around at all hours of the night—and in such ridiculous clothes. She must be out of her mind."

Miriam got up and moved to a corner where a covered birdcage hung from a ceiling chain. She peeked beneath the cover. "It's a canary," she said. "Would you mind if I woke him? I'd like to hear him sing."

"Leave Tommy alone," said Mrs. Miller anxiously. "Don't you dare wake him."

"Certainly," said Miriam. "But I don't see why I can't hear him sing." And then, "Have you anything to eat? I'm starving! Even milk and a jam sandwich would be fine."

"Look," said Mrs. Miller, arising from the hassock, "look—if I make some nice sandwiches will you be a good child and run along home? It's past midnight, I'm sure."

"It's snowing," reproached Miriam. "And cold and dark."

"Well, you shouldn't have come here to begin with," said Mrs. Miller, struggling to control her voice. "I can't help the weather. If you want anything to eat, you'll have to promise to leave."

Miriam brushed a braid against her cheek. Her eyes were thoughtful, as if weighing the proposition. She turned toward the birdcage. "Very well," she said, "I promise."

—

How old is she? Ten? Eleven? Mrs. Miller, in the kitchen, unsealed a jar of strawberry preserves and cut four slices of bread. She poured a glass of milk and paused to light a cigarette. *And why has she come?* Her hand shook as she held the match, fascinated, till it burned her finger. The canary was singing; singing as he did in the morning and at no other time. "Miriam," she called, "Miriam, I told you not to disturb Tommy." There was no answer. She called again; all she heard was the canary. She inhaled the cigarette and discovered she had lighted the cork-tip end and—oh, really, she mustn't lose her temper.

She carried the food in on a tray and set it on the coffee table. She saw first that the birdcage still wore its night cover. And Tommy was singing. It gave her a queer sensation. And no one was in the room. Mrs. Miller went through an alcove leading to her bedroom; at the door she caught her breath.

She studied Mrs. Miller, forcing their eyes to meet.

"What are you doing?" she asked.

Miriam glanced up and in her eyes there was a look that was not ordinary. She was standing by the bureau, a jewel case opened before her. For a minute she studied Mrs. Miller, forcing their eyes to meet, and she smiled. "There's nothing good here," she said. "But I like this." Her hand held a cameo brooch. "It's charming."

"Suppose—perhaps you'd better put it back," said Mrs. Miller, feeling suddenly the need of some support. She leaned against the door frame; her head was unbearably heavy; a pressure weighted the rhythm of her heartbeat. The light seemed to flutter defectively. "Please, child—a gift from my husband. . . ."

"But it's beautiful and I want it," said Miriam. *"Give it to me."*

As she stood, striving to shape a sentence which would somehow save the brooch, it came to Mrs. Miller there was no one to whom she might turn; she was alone; a fact that had not been among her thoughts for a long time. Its sheer emphasis was stunning. But here in her own room in the hushed snow-city were evidences she could not ignore or, she knew with startling clarity, resist.

—

Miriam ate ravenously, and when the sandwiches and milk were gone, her fingers made cobweb movements over the plate, gathering crumbs. The cameo gleamed on her blouse, the blond profile like a trick reflection of its wearer. "That was very nice," she sighed, "though now an almond cake or a cherry would be ideal. Sweets are lovely, don't you think?"

Mrs. Miller was perched precariously on the hassock, smoking a cigarette. Her hairnet had slipped lopsided and loose strands straggled down her face. Her eyes were stupidly concentrated on nothing and her cheeks were mottled in red patches, as though a fierce slap had left permanent marks.

"Is there a candy—a cake?"

Mrs. Miller tapped ash on the rug. Her head swayed slightly as she tried to focus her eyes. "You promised to leave if I made the sandwiches," she said.

"Dear me, did I?"

"It was a promise and I'm tired and I don't feel well at all."

"Mustn't fret," said Miriam. "I'm only teasing."

She picked up her coat, slung it over her arm, and arranged her beret in front of a mirror. Presently she bent close to Mrs. Miller and whispered, "Kiss me good night."

"Please—I'd rather not," said Mrs. Miller.

Miriam lifted a shoulder, arched an eyebrow. "As you like," she said, and went directly to the coffee table, seized the vase containing the paper roses, carried it to where the hard surface of the floor lay bare, and hurled it downward. Glass sprayed in all directions and she stamped her foot on the bouquet.

Then slowly she walked to the door, but before closing it, she looked back at Mrs. Miller with a slyly innocent curiosity.

—

Mrs. Miller spent the next day in bed, rising once to feed the canary and drink a cup of tea; she took her temperature and had none, yet her dreams were feverishly agitated; their unbalanced mood lingered even as she lay staring wide-eyed at the ceiling. One dream threaded through the others like an elusively mysterious theme in a complicated symphony, and the scenes it depicted were sharply outlined, as though sketched by a hand of gifted intensity: a small girl, wearing a bridal gown and a wreath of leaves, led a gray procession down a mountain path, and among them there was unusual silence till a woman at the rear asked, "Where is she taking us?" "No one knows," said an old man marching in front. "But isn't she pretty?" volunteered a third voice. "Isn't she like a frost flower . . . so shining and white?"

Tuesday morning she woke up feeling better; harsh slats of sunlight, slanting through Venetian blinds, shed a disrupting light on her unwholesome fancies. She opened the window to discover a thawed, mild-as-spring day; a sweep of clean new clouds crumpled against a vastly blue, out-of-season sky; and across the low line of rooftops she could see the river and smoke curving from tugboat stacks in a warm wind. A great silver truck plowed the snow-banked street, its machine sound humming on the air.

After straightening the apartment, she went to the grocer's, cashed a check and continued to Schrafft's, where she ate breakfast and chatted happily with the waitress. Oh, it was a wonderful day—more like a holiday—and it would be so foolish to go home.

She boarded a Lexington Avenue bus and rode up to Eighty-sixth Street; it was here that she had decided to do a little shopping.

She had no idea what she wanted or needed, but she idled along, intent only upon the passers-by, brisk and preoccupied, who gave her a disturbing sense of separateness.

It was while waiting at the corner of Third Avenue that she saw the man: an old man, bowlegged and stooped under an armload of bulging packages; he wore a shabby brown coat and a checkered cap. Suddenly she realized they were exchanging a smile: there was nothing friendly about this smile, it was merely two cold flickers of recognition. But she was certain she had never seen him before.

He was standing next to an El pillar, and as she crossed the street he turned and followed. He kept quite close; from the corner of her eye she watched his reflection wavering on the shopwindows.

Then in the middle of the block she stopped and faced him. He stopped also and cocked his head, grinning. But what could she say? Do? Here, in broad daylight, on Eighty-sixth Street? It was useless and, despising her own helplessness, she quickened her steps.

Now Second Avenue is a dismal street, made from scraps and ends; part cobblestone, part asphalt, part cement; and its atmosphere of desertion is permanent. Mrs. Miller walked five blocks without meeting anyone, and all the while the steady crunch of his footfalls in the snow stayed near. And when she came to a florist's shop, the sound was still with her. She hurried inside and watched through the glass door as the old man passed; he kept his eyes straight ahead and didn't slow his pace, but he did one strange, telling thing: he tipped his cap.

—

"Six white ones, did you say?" asked the florist. "Yes," she told him, "white roses." From there she went to a glassware store and selected a vase, presumably a replacement for the one Miriam had broken, though the price was intolerable and the vase itself (she thought) grotesquely vulgar. But a series of unaccountable purchases had begun, as if by prearranged plan: a plan of which she had not the least knowledge or control.

She bought a bag of glazed cherries, and at a place called the Knickerbocker Bakery she paid forty cents for six almond cakes.

Within the last hour the weather had turned cold again; like blurred lenses, winter clouds cast a shade over the sun, and the skeleton of an early dusk colored the sky; a damp mist mixed with the wind and the voices of a few children who romped high on mountains of gutter snow seemed lonely and cheerless. Soon the first flake fell, and when Mrs. Miller reached the brownstone house, snow was falling in a swift screen and foot tracks vanished as they were printed.

—

The white roses were arranged decoratively in the vase. The glazed cherries shone on a ceramic plate. The almond cakes, dusted with sugar, awaited a hand. The canary fluttered on its swing and picked at a bar of seed.

At precisely five the doorbell rang. Mrs. Miller *knew* who it was. The hem of her housecoat trailed as she crossed the floor. "Is that you?" she called.

"Naturally," said Miriam, the word resounding shrilly from the hall. "Open this door."

"Go away," said Mrs. Miller.

"Please hurry . . . I have a heavy package."

"Go away," said Mrs. Miller. She returned to the living room, lighted a cigarette, sat down and calmly listened to the buzzer; on and on and on. "You might as well leave. I have no intention of letting you in."

Shortly the bell stopped. For possibly ten minutes Mrs. Miller did not move. Then, hearing no sound, she concluded Miriam had gone. She tiptoed to the door and opened it a sliver; Miriam was half-reclining atop a cardboard box with a beautiful French doll cradled in her arms.

"Really, I thought you were never coming," she said peevishly. "Here, help me get this in, it's awfully heavy."

It was not spell-like compulsion that Mrs. Miller felt, but rather a curious passivity; she brought in the box, Miriam, the doll. Miriam curled up on the sofa, not troubling to remove her coat or beret, and watched disinterestedly as Mrs. Miller dropped the box and stood trembling, trying to catch her breath.

"Thank you," she said. In the daylight she looked pinched and drawn, her hair less luminous. The French doll she was loving wore an exquisite powdered wig and its idiot glass eyes sought solace in Miriam's. "I have a surprise," she continued. "Look into my box."

Kneeling, Mrs. Miller parted the flaps and lifted out another doll; then a blue dress which she recalled as the one Miriam had worn that first night at the theater; and of the remainder she said, "It's all clothes. Why?"

"Because I've come to live with you," said Miriam, twisting a cherry stem. "Wasn't it nice of you to buy me the cherries . . . ?"

"But you can't! For God's sake go away—go away and leave me alone!"

". . . and the roses and the almond cakes? How really wonderfully generous. You know, these cherries are delicious. The last place I lived was with an old man; he was terribly poor and we never had good things to eat. But I think I'll be happy here." She paused to snuggle her doll closer. "Now, if you'll just show me where to put my things . . ."

Mrs. Miller's face dissolved into a mask of ugly red lines; she began to cry, and it was an unnatural, tearless sort of weeping, as though, not having wept for a long time, she had forgotten how. Carefully she edged backward till she touched the door.

—

She fumbled through the hall and down the stairs to a landing below. She pounded frantically on the door of the first apartment she came to; a short, redheaded man answered and she pushed past him. "Say, what the hell is this?" he said. "Anything wrong, lover?" asked a young woman who appeared from the kitchen, drying her hands. And it was to her that Mrs. Miller turned.

"Listen," she cried, "I'm ashamed behaving this way but—well, I'm Mrs. H. T. Miller and I live upstairs and . . ." She pressed her hands over her face. "It sounds so absurd. . . ."

The woman guided her to a chair, while the man excitedly rattled pocket change. "Yeah?"

"I live upstairs and there's a little girl visiting me, and I suppose that I'm afraid of her. She won't leave and I can't make her and—she's going to do something terrible. She's already stolen my cameo, but she's about to do something worse—something terrible!"

The man asked, "Is she a relative, huh?"

Mrs. Miller shook her head. "I don't know who she is. Her name's Miriam, but I don't know for certain who she is."

"You gotta calm down, honey," said the woman, stroking Mrs. Miller's arm. "Harry here'll tend to this kid. Go on, lover." And Mrs. Miller said, "The door's open—5A."

After the man left, the woman brought a towel and bathed Mrs. Miller's face. "You're very kind," Mrs. Miller said. "I'm sorry to act like such a fool, only this wicked child . . ."

"Sure, honey," consoled the woman. "Now, you better take it easy."

Mrs. Miller rested her head in the crook of her arm; she was quiet enough to be asleep. The woman turned a radio dial; a piano and a husky voice filled the silence and the woman, tapping her foot, kept excellent time. "Maybe we oughta go up too," she said.

"I don't want to see her again. I don't want to be anywhere near her."

"Uh huh, but what you shoulda done, you shoulda called a cop."

Presently they heard the man on the stairs. He strode into the room frowning and scratching the back of his neck. "Nobody there," he said, honestly embarrassed. "She musta beat it."

"Harry, you're a jerk," announced the woman. "We been sitting here the whole time and we woulda seen . . ." she stopped abruptly, for the man's glance was sharp.

"I looked all over," he said, "and there just ain't nobody there. Nobody, understand?"

"Tell me," said Mrs. Miller, rising, "tell me, did you see a large box? Or a doll?"

"No, ma'am, I didn't."

And the woman, as if delivering a verdict, said, "Well, for cryinoutloud. . . ."

—

Mrs. Miller entered her apartment softly; she walked to the center of the room and stood quite still. No, in a sense it had not changed: the roses, the cakes, and the cherries were in place. But this was an empty room, emptier than if the furnishings and familiars were not present, lifeless and petrified as a funeral parlor. The sofa loomed before her with a new strangeness: its vacancy had a meaning that would have been less penetrating and terrible had Miriam been curled on it. She gazed fixedly at the space where she remembered setting the box and, for a moment, the hassock spun desperately. And she looked through the window; surely the river was real, surely snow was falling—but then, one could not be certain witness to anything: Miriam, so vividly there—and yet, where was she? Where, where?

As though moving in a dream, she sank to a chair. The room was losing shape; it was dark and getting darker and there was nothing to be done about it; she could not lift her hand to a light a lamp.

Suddenly, closing her eyes, she felt an upward surge, like a diver emerging from some deeper, greener depth. In times of terror or immense distress, there are moments when the mind waits, as though for a revelation, while a skein of calm is woven over thought; it is like a sleep, or a supernatural trance; and during this lull one is aware of a force of quiet reasoning: well, what if she had never really known a girl named Miriam? That she had been foolishly frightened on the street? In the end, like everything else, it was of no importance. For the only thing she had lost to Miriam was her identity, but now she knew she had found again the person who lived in this room, who cooked her own meals, who owned a canary, who was someone she could trust and believe in: Mrs. H. T. Miller.

Listening in contentment, she became aware of a double sound: a bureau drawer opening and closing; she seemed to hear it long after completion—opening and closing. Then gradually, the harshness of it was replaced by the murmur of a silk dress and this, delicately faint, was moving nearer and swelling in intensity till the walls trembled with the vibration and the room was caving under a wave of whisper. Mrs. Miller stiffened and opened her eyes to a dull, direct stare.

"Hello," said Miriam.

The Tell-Tale Heart

By Edgar Allan Poe

TRUE!—NERVOUS—very, very dreadfully nervous I had been and am; but why will you say that I am mad? The disease had sharpened my senses—not destroyed—not dulled them. Above all was the sense of hearing acute. I heard all things in the heaven and in the earth. I heard many things in hell. How, then, am I mad? Hearken! and observe how healthily—how calmly I can tell you the whole story.

It is impossible to say how first the idea entered my brain; but once conceived, it haunted me day and night. Object there was none. Passion there was none. I loved the old man. He had never wronged me. He had never given me insult. For his gold I had no desire. I think it was his eye! yes, it was this! He had the eye of a vulture—a pale blue eye, with a film over it. Whenever it fell upon me, my blood ran cold; and so by degrees—very gradually—I made up my mind to take the life of the old man, and thus rid myself of the eye forever.

Now this is the point. You fancy me mad. Madmen know nothing. But you should have seen me. You should have seen how wisely I proceeded—with what caution—with what foresight—with what dissimulation I went to work! I was never kinder to the old man than during the whole week before I killed him. And every night, about midnight, I turned the latch of his door and opened it—oh so gently! And then, when I had made an opening sufficient for my head, I put in a dark lantern, all closed, closed, that no light shone out, and then I thrust in my head. Oh, you would have laughed to see how cunningly I thrust it in! I moved it slowly—very, very slowly, so that I might not disturb the old man's sleep. It took me an hour to place my whole head within the opening so far that I could see him as he lay upon his bed. Ha! would a madman have been so wise as this, And then, when my head was well in the room, I undid the lantern cautiously—oh, so cautiously—cautiously (for the hinges creaked)—I undid it just so much that a single thin ray fell upon the vulture eye. And this I did for seven long nights—every night just at midnight—but I found the eye always closed; and so it was impossible to do the work; for it was not the old man who vexed me, but his Evil Eye. And every morning, when the day broke, I went boldly into the chamber, and spoke courageously to him, calling him by name in a hearty tone, and inquiring how he has passed the night. So you see he would have been a very profound old man, indeed, to suspect that every night, just at twelve, I looked in upon him while he slept.

Upon the eighth night I was more than usually cautious in opening the door. A watch's minute hand moves more quickly than did mine. Never before that night had I felt the extent of my own powers—of my sagacity. I could scarcely contain my feelings of triumph. To think that there I was, opening the door, little by little, and he not even to dream of my secret deeds or thoughts. I fairly chuckled at the idea; and perhaps he heard me; for he moved on the bed suddenly, as if startled. Now you may think that I drew back—but no. His room was as black as pitch with the thick darkness (for the shutters were close fastened, through fear of robbers), and so I knew that he could not see the opening of the door, and I kept pushing it on steadily, steadily.

I had my head in, and was about to open the lantern, when my thumb slipped upon the tin fastening, and the old man sprang up in bed, crying out—"Who's there?"

I kept quite still and said nothing. For a whole hour I did not move a muscle, and in the meantime I did not hear him lie down. He was still sitting up in the bed listening—just as I have done, night after night, hearkening to the death watches in the wall.

Presently I heard a slight groan, and I knew it was the groan of mortal terror. It was not a groan of pain or of grief—oh, no!—it was the low stifled sound that arises from the bottom of the soul when overcharged with awe. I knew the sound well. Many a night, just at midnight, when all the world slept, it has welled up from my own bosom, deepening, with its dreadful echo, the terrors that distracted me. I say I knew it well. I knew what the old man felt, and pitied him, although I chuckled at heart. I knew that he had been lying awake ever since the first slight noise, when he had turned in the bed. His fears had been ever since growing upon him. He had been trying to fancy them causeless, but could not. He had been saying to himself—"It is nothing but the wind in the chimney—it is only a mouse crossing the floor," or "It is merely a cricket which has made a single chirp." Yes, he had been trying to comfort himself with these suppositions: but he had found all in vain. All in vain; because Death, in approaching him had stalked with his black shadow before him, and enveloped the victim. And it was the mournful influence of the unperceived shadow that caused him to feel—although he neither saw nor heard—to feel the presence of my head within the room.

When I had waited a long time, very patiently, without hearing him lie down, I resolved to open a little—a very, very little crevice in the lantern. So I opened it—you cannot imagine how stealthily, stealthily—until, at length a simple dim ray, like the thread of the spider, shot from out the crevice and fell full upon the vulture eye.

It was open—wide, wide open—and I grew furious as I gazed upon it. I saw it with perfect distinctness—all a dull blue, with a hideous veil over it that chilled the very marrow in my bones; but I could see nothing else of the old man's face or person: for I had directed the ray as if by instinct, precisely upon the damned spot.

And have I not told you that what you mistake for madness is but over-acuteness of the sense?—now, I say, there came to my ears a low, dull, quick sound, such as a watch makes when enveloped in cotton. I knew that sound well, too. It was the beating of the old man's heart. It increased my fury, as the beating of a drum stimulates the soldier into courage.

But even yet I refrained and kept still. I scarcely breathed. I held the lantern motionless. I tried how steadily I could maintain the ray upon the eye. Meantime the hellish tattoo of the heart increased. It grew quicker and quicker, and louder and louder every instant. The old man's terror must have been extreme! It grew louder, I say, louder every moment!—do you mark me well I have told you that I am nervous: so I am. And now at the dead hour of the night, amid the dreadful silence of that old house, so strange a noise as this excited me to uncontrollable terror. Yet, for some minutes longer I refrained and stood still. But the beating grew louder, louder! I thought the heart must burst. And now a new anxiety seized me—the sound would be heard by a neighbor! The old man's hour had come! With a loud yell, I threw open the lantern and leaped into the room. He shrieked once—once only. In an instant I dragged him to the floor, and pulled the heavy bed over him. I then smiled gaily, to find the deed so far done. But, for many minutes, the heart beat on with a muffled sound. This, however, did not vex me; it would not be heard through the wall. At length it ceased. The old man was dead. I removed the bed and examined the corpse. Yes, he was stone, stone dead. I placed my hand upon the heart and held it there many minutes. There was no pulsation. He was stone dead. His eye would trouble me no more.

If still you think me mad, you will think so no longer when I describe the wise precautions I took for the concealment of the body. The night waned, and I worked hastily, but in silence. First of all I dismembered the corpse. I cut off the head and the arms and the legs.

I then took up three planks from the flooring of the chamber, and deposited all between the scantlings. I then replaced the boards so cleverly, so cunningly, that no human eye—not even his—could have detected any thing wrong. There was nothing to wash out—no stain of any kind—no blood-spot whatever. I had been too wary for that. A tub had caught all—ha! ha!

When I had made an end of these labors, it was four o'clock—still dark as midnight. As the bell sounded the hour, there came a knocking at the street door. I went down to open it with a light heart,—for what had I now to fear? There entered three men, who introduced themselves, with perfect suavity, as officers of the police. A shriek had been heard by a neighbor during the night; suspicion of foul play had been aroused; information had been lodged at the police office, and they (the officers) had been deputed to search the premises.

I smiled,—for what had I to fear? I bade the gentlemen welcome. The shriek, I said, was my own in a dream. The old man, I mentioned, was absent in the country. I took my visitors all over the house. I bade them search—search well. I led them, at length, to his chamber. I showed them his treasures,

The old man was dead.

secure, undisturbed. In the enthusiasm of my confidence, I brought chairs into the room, and desired them here to rest from their fatigues, while I myself, in the wild audacity of my perfect triumph, placed my own seat upon the very spot beneath which reposed the corpse of the victim.

The officers were satisfied. My manner had convinced them. I was singularly at ease. They sat, and while I answered cheerily, they chatted of familiar things. But, ere long, I felt myself getting pale and wished them gone. My head ached, and I fancied a ringing in my ears: but still they sat and still chatted. The ringing became more distinct:—It continued and became more distinct: I talked more freely to get rid of the feeling: but it continued and gained definiteness—until, at length, I found that the noise was not within my ears.

No doubt I now grew very pale;—but I talked more fluently, and with a heightened voice. Yet the sound increased—and what could I do? It was a low, dull, quick sound—much such a sound as a watch makes when enveloped in cotton. I gasped for breath—and yet the officers heard it not. I talked more quickly—more vehemently; but the noise steadily increased. I arose and argued about trifles, in a high key and with violent gesticulations; but the noise steadily increased. Why would they not be gone? I paced the floor to and fro with heavy strides, as if excited to fury by the observations of the men—but the noise steadily increased. Oh God! what could I do? I foamed—I raved—I swore! I swung the chair upon which I had been sitting, and grated it upon the boards, but the noise arose over all and continually increased. It grew louder—louder—louder! And still the men chatted pleasantly, and smiled. Was it possible they heard not? Almighty God!—no, no! They heard!—they suspected!—they knew!—they were making a mockery of my horror!—this I thought, and this I think. But anything was better than this agony! Anything was more tolerable than this derision! I could bear those hypocritical smiles no longer! I felt that I must scream or die! and now—again!—hark! louder! louder! louder! louder!

"Villains!" I shrieked, "dissemble no more! I admit the deed!—tear up the planks! here, here!—It is the beating of his hideous heart!"

Genesis and Catastrophe (A True Story)

By Roald Dahl

"Everything is normal," the doctor was saying. "Just lie back and relax." His voice was miles away in the distance and he seemed to be shouting at her. "You have a son."

"What?"

"You have a fine son. You understand that, don't you? A fine son. Did you hear him crying?"

"Is he all right, Doctor?"

"Of course he is all right."

"Please let me see him."

"You'll see him in a moment."

"You are certain he is all right?"

"I am quite certain."

"Is he still crying?"

"Try to rest. There is nothing to worry about."

"Why has he stopped crying, Doctor? What happened?"

"Don't excite yourself, please. Everything is normal."

"I want to see him. Please let me see him."

"Dear lady," the doctor said, patting her hand. "You have a fine strong healthy child. Don't you believe me when I tell you that?"

"What is the woman over there doing to him?"

"Your baby is being made to look pretty for you," the doctor said. "We are giving him a little wash, that is all. You must spare us a moment or two for that."

"You swear he is all right?"

"I swear it. Now lie back and relax. Close your eyes. Go on, close your eyes. That's right. That's better. Good girl . . ."

"I have prayed and prayed that he will live, Doctor."

"Of course he will live. What are you talking about?"

"The others didn't."

"What?"

"None of my other ones lived, Doctor."

The doctor stood beside the bed looking down at the pale exhausted face of the young woman. He had never seen her before today. She and her husband were new people in the town. The innkeeper's wife, who had come up to assist in the delivery, had told him that the husband worked at the local customs-house on the border and that the two of them had arrived quite suddenly at the inn with one trunk and one suitcase about three months ago. The husband was a drunkard, the innkeeper's wife had said, an arrogant, overbearing, bullying little drunkard, but the young woman was gentle and religious. And she was very sad. She never smiled. In the few weeks that she had been here, the innkeeper's wife had never once seen her smile. Also there was a rumor that this was the husband's third marriage, that one wife had died and that the other had divorced him for unsavory reasons. But that was only a rumor.

The doctor bent down and pulled the sheet up a little higher over the patient's chest. "You have nothing to worry about," he said gently. "This is a perfectly normal baby."

"That's exactly what they told me about the others. But I lost all three of my children, so you mustn't blame me for being anxious."

"Three?"

"This is my fourth . . . in four years."

The doctor shifted his feet uneasily on the bare floor.

"I don't think you know what it means, Doctor, to lose them all, all three of them, slowly, separately, one by one. I keep seeing them. I can see Gustav's face now as clearly as if he were lying here beside me in the bed. Gustav was a lovely boy, Doctor. But he was always ill. It is terrible when they are always ill and there is nothing you can do to help them."

"I know."

The woman opened her eyes, stared up at the doctor for a few seconds, then closed them again.

"My little girl was called Ida. She died a few days before Christmas. That is only four months ago. I just wish you could have seen Ida, Doctor."

"You have a new one now."

"But Ida was so beautiful."

"Yes," the doctor said. "I know."

"How can you know?" she cried.

"I am sure that she was a lovely child. But this new one is also like that." The doctor turned away from the bed and walked over to the window and stood there looking out. It was a wet gray April afternoon, and across the street he could see the red roofs of the houses and the huge raindrops splashing on the tiles.

"Ida was two years old, Doctor . . . and she was so beautiful I was never able to take my eyes off her from the time I dressed her in the morning until she was safe in bed again at night. I used to live in holy terror of something happening to that child. Gustav had gone and my little Otto had also gone and she was all I had left. Sometimes I used to get up in the night and creep over to the cradle and put my ear close to her mouth just to make sure that she was breathing."

"Try to rest," the doctor said, going back to the bed. "Please try to rest." The woman's face was white and bloodless, and there was slight bluish-gray tinge around the nostrils and the mouth. A few strands of damp hair hung down over her forehead, sticking to the skin.

"When she died, I was already pregnant again when that happened, Doctor. This new one was a good four months on its way when Ida died. 'I don't want it!' I shouted after the funeral. 'I won't have it! I have buried enough children!' And my husband, he was strolling among the guests with a big glass of beer in his hand . . . he turned around quickly and said, 'I have news for you, Klara, I have good news.' Can you imagine that, Doctor? We have just buried our third child and he stands there with a glass of beer in his hand and tells me that he has good news. 'Today I have been posted to Braunau,' he says, 'so you can start packing at once. This will be a new start for you, Klara,' he says. 'It will be a new place and you can have a new doctor. . . .'"

"Please don't talk any more."

"You *are* the new doctor, aren't you, Doctor?"

"That's right."

"And here we are in Braunau."

"Yes."

"I am frightened, Doctor."

"Try not to be frightened."

"What chance can the fourth one have now?"

"You must stop thinking like that."

"I can't help it. I am certain there is something inherited that causes my children to die in this way. There must be."

"That is nonsense."

"Do you know what my husband said to me when Otto was born, Doctor? He came into the room and he looked into the cradle where Otto was lying and he said, 'Why do all my children have to be so small and weak?'"

"I am sure he didn't say that."

"He put his head right into Otto's cradle as though he were examining a tiny insect and he said, 'All I am saying is why can't they be better *specimens?* That's all I am saying.' And three days after that Otto was dead. We baptized him quickly on the third and he died the same evening. And then Gustav died. And then Ida died. All of them died, Doctor . . . and suddenly the whole house was empty. . . ."

"Don't think about it now."

"Is this one so very small?"

"He is a normal child."

"But small?"

"He is a little small, perhaps. But the small ones are often a lot tougher than the big ones. Just imagine, Frau Hitler, this time next year he will be almost learning how to walk. Isn't that a lovely thought?"

She didn't answer this.

"And two years from now he will probably be talking his head off and driving you crazy with his chatter. Have you settled on a name for him yet?"

"A name?"

"Yes."

"I don't know. I'm not sure. I think my husband said that if it was a boy we were going to call him Adolfus."

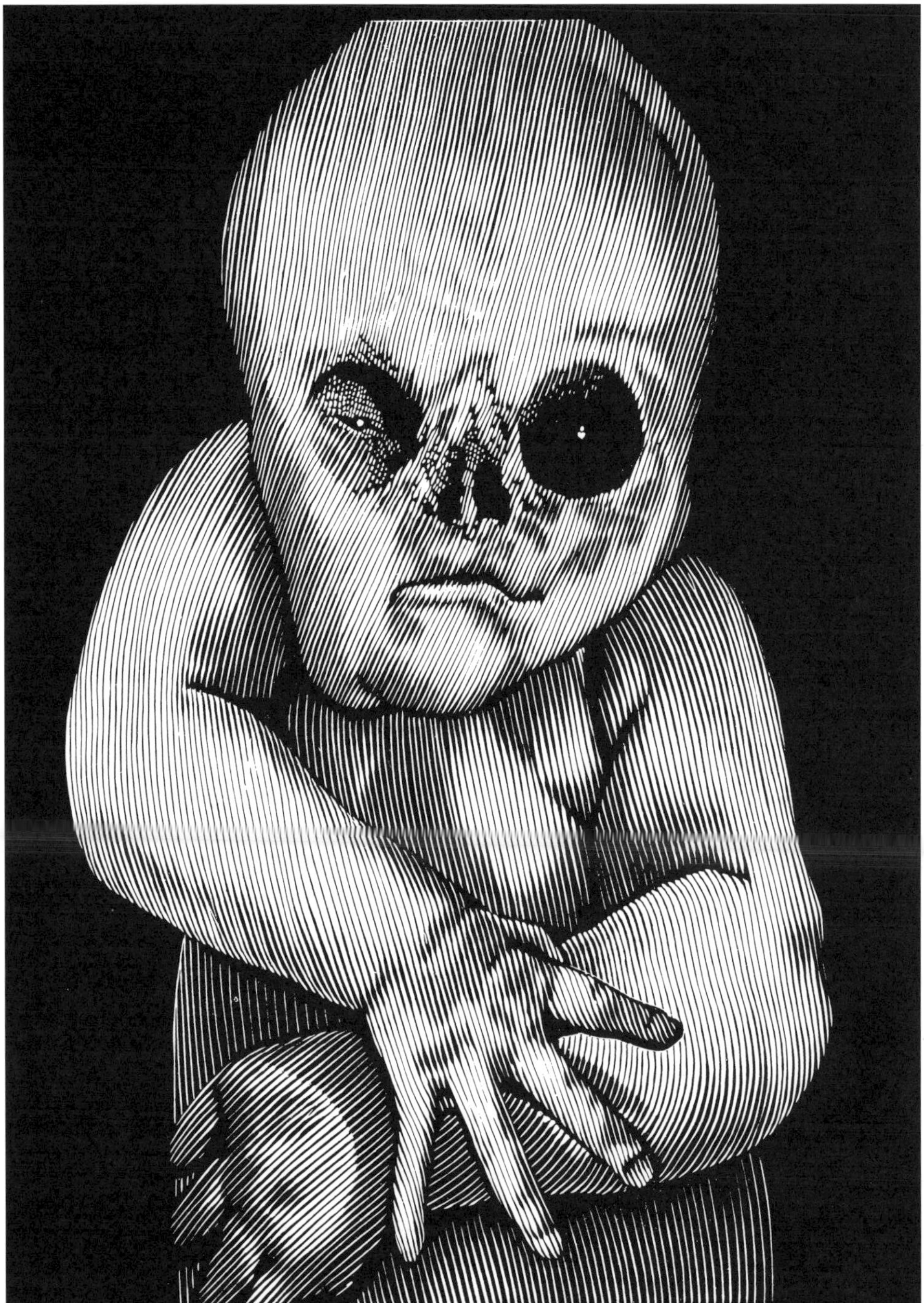

Here is the little beauty!

"That means he would be called Adolf."

"Yes. My husband likes Adolf because it has a certain similarity to Alois. My husband is called Alois."

"Excellent."

"Oh, no!" she cried, starting up suddenly from the pillow. "That's the same question they asked me when Otto was born! It means he is going to die! You are going to baptize him at once!"

"Now, now," the doctor said, taking her gently by the shoulders. "You are quite wrong. I promise you you are wrong. I was simply being an inquisitive old man, that is all. I love talking about names. I think Adolfus is a particularly fine name. It is one of my favorites. And look—here he comes now."

The innkeeper's wife, carrying the baby high up on her enormous bosom, came sailing across the room towards the bed. "Here is the little beauty!" she cried, beaming. "Would you like to hold him, my dear? Shall I put him beside you?"

"Is he well wrapped?" the doctor asked. "It is extremely cold in here."

"Certainly he is well wrapped."

The baby was tightly swaddled in a white woolen shawl, and only the tiny pink head protruded. The innkeeper's wife placed him gently on the bed beside the mother. "There you are," she said. "Now you can lie there and look at him to your heart's content."

"I think you will like him," the doctor said, smiling. "He is a fine little baby."

"He has the most lovely hands!" the innkeeper's wife exclaimed. "Such long delicate fingers!"

The mother didn't move. She didn't even turn her head to look.

"Go on!" cried the innkeeper's wife." "He won't bite you!"

"I am frightened to look. I don't dare to believe that I have another baby and that he is all right."

"Don't be so stupid."

Slowly, the mother turned her head and looked at the small, incredibly serene face that lay on the pillow beside her.

"Is this my baby?"

"Of course."

"Oh . . . oh . . . but he is beautiful."

The doctor turned away and went over to the table and began putting his things into his bag. The mother lay on the bed gazing at the child and smiling and touching him and making little noises of pleasure. "Hello, Adolfus," she whispered. "Hello, my little Adolf . . ."

"Ssshh!" said the innkeeper's wife. "Listen! I think your husband is coming."

The doctor walked over to the door and opened it and looked out into the corridor.

"Herr Hitler?"

"Yes."

"Come in, please."

A small man in a dark-green uniform stepped softly into the room and looked around him.

"Congratulations," the doctor said. "You have a son."

The man had a pair of enormous whiskers meticulously groomed after the manner of the Emperor Franz Josef, and he smelled strongly of beer. "A son?"

"Yes."

"How is he?"

"He is fine. So is your wife."

"Good." The father turned and walked with a curious little prancing stride over to the bed where his wife was lying. "Well, Klara," he said, smiling through his whiskers. "How did it go?" He bent down to take a look at the baby. Then he bent lower. In a series of quick jerky movements, he bent lower and lower until his face was only about twelve inches from the baby's head. The wife lay sideways on the pillow, staring up at him with a kind of supplicating look.

"He has the most marvelous pair of lungs," the innkeeper's wife announced. "You should have heard him screaming just after he came into this world."

"But my God, Klara . . ."

"What is it, dear?"

"This one is even smaller than Otto was!"

The doctor took a couple of quick paces forward. "There is nothing wrong with that child," he said.

Slowly, the husband straightened up and turned away from the bed and looked at the doctor. He seemed bewildered and stricken. "It's no good lying, Doctor," he said. "I know what it means. It's going to be the same all over again."

"Now you listen to me," the doctor said.

"But do you *know* what happened to the others, Doctor?"

"You must forget about the others, Herr Hitler. Give this one a chance."

"But so small and weak!"

"My dear sir, he has only just been born."

"Even so . . ."

"What are you trying to do?" cried the innkeeper's wife. "Talk him into his grave?"

"That's enough!" the doctor said sharply.

The mother was weeping now. Great sobs were shaking her body.

The doctor walked over to the husband and put a hand on his shoulder. "Be good to her," he whispered. "Please. It is very important." Then he squeezed the husband's shoulder hard and began pushing him forward surreptitiously to the edge of the bed. The husband hesitated. The doctor squeezed harder, signaling to him urgently through fingers and thumb. At last, reluctantly, the husband bent down and kissed his wife lightly on the cheek.

"All right, Klara," he said. "Now stop crying."

"I have prayed so hard that he will live, Alois."

"Yes."

"Every day for months I have gone to the church and begged on my knees that this one will be allowed to live."

"Yes, Klara, I know."

"Three dead children is all that I can stand, don't you realize that?"

"Of course."

"He *must* live, Alois. He *must,* he *must* . . . Oh God, be merciful unto him now. . . .

The Squaw

By Bram Stoker

Nurnberg at the time was not so much exploited as it has been since then. Irving had not been playing Faust, and the very name of the old town was hardly known to the great bulk of the traveling public. My wife and I being in the second week of our honeymoon, naturally wanted someone else to join our party, so that when the cheery stranger, Elias P. Hutcheson, hailing from Isthmian City, Bleeding Gulch, Maple Tree County, Neb., turned up at the station at Frankfort, and casually remarked that he was going on to see the most all-fired old Methuselah of a town in Yurrup, and that he guessed that so much traveling alone was enough to send an intelligent, active citizen into the melancholy ward of a daft house, we took the pretty broad hint and suggested that we should join forces. We found, on comparing notes afterwards, that we had each intended to speak with some diffidence or hesitation so as not to appear too eager, such not being a good compliment to the success of our married life; but the effect was entirely marred by our both beginning to speak at the same instant—stopping simultaneously and then going on together again. Anyhow, no matter how, it was done; and Elias P. Hutcheson became one of our party. Straightway Amelia and I found the pleasant benefit; instead of quarrelling, as we had been doing, we found that the restraining influence of a third party was such that we now took every opportunity of spooning in odd corners. Amelia declares that ever since she has, as the result of that experience, advised all her friends to take a friend on the honeymoon. Well, we "did" Nurnberg together, and much enjoyed the racy remarks of our transatlantic friend, who, from his quaint speech and his wonderful stock of adventures, might have stepped out of a novel. We kept for the last object of interest in the city to be visited the Burg, and on the day appointed for the visit strolled round the outer wall of the city by the eastern side.

The Burg is seated on a rock dominating the town and an immensely deep fosse guards it on the northern side. Nurnberg has been happy in that it was never sacked; had it been it would certainly not be so spick-and-span perfect as it is at present. The ditch has not been used for centuries, and now its base is spread with tea gardens and orchards, of which some of the trees are of quite respectable growth. As we wandered round the wall, dawdling in the hot July sunshine, we often paused to admire the views spread before us, and in especial the great plain covered with towns and villages and bounded with a blue line of hills, like a landscape of Claude Lorraine. From this we always turned with new delight to the city itself, with its myriad of quaint old gables and acre wide red roofs dotted with dormer windows, tier upon tier. A little to our right rose the towers of the Burg, and nearer still, standing grim, the Torture Tower, which was, and is, perhaps, the most interesting place in the city. For centuries the tradition of the Iron Virgin of Nurnberg has been handed down as an instance of the horrors of cruelty of which man is capable; we had long looked forward to seeing it; and here at last was its home.

In one of our pauses we leaned over the wall of the moat and looked down. The garden seemed quite fifty or sixty feet below us, and the sun pouring into it with an intense, moveless heat like that of an oven. Beyond rose the gray, grim wall seemingly of endless height, and losing itself right and left in the angles of bastion and counterscarp. Trees and bushes crowned the wall, and above again towered the lofty houses on whose massive beauty time has only set the hand of approval. The sun was hot and we were lazy; time was our own, and we lingered, leaning on the wall. Just below us was a pretty sight—a great black cat lying stretched in the sun, while round her gamboled prettily a tiny black kitten. The mother would wave her tail for the kitten to play with, or would raise her feet and push away the little one as an encouragement to further play. They were just at the foot of the wall, and Elias P. Hutcheson, in order to help the play, stooped and took from the walk a moderate sized pebble.

"See!" he said, "I will drop it near the kitten, and they will both wonder where it came from."

"Oh, be careful," said my wife; "you might hit the dear little thing!"

"Not me, ma'am," said Elias P. "Why, I'm as tender as a Maine cherry tree. Lor, bless ye, I wouldn't hurt the poor pooty little critter more'n I'd scalp a baby. An' you may bet your variegated socks on that! See, I'll drop it fur away on the outside so's not to go near her!" Thus saying, he leaned over and held his arm out at full length and dropped the stone. It may be that there is some attractive force which draws lesser matters to greater; or more probably that the wall was not plump but sloped to its base—we not noticing the inclination from above; but the stone fell with a sickening thud that came up to us through the hot air, right on the kitten's head, and shattered out its little brains then and there. The black cat cast a swift upward glance, and we saw her eyes like green fire fixed an instant on Elias P. Hutcheson; and then her attention was given to the kitten, which lay still with just a quiver of her tiny limbs, while a thin red stream trickled from a gaping wound. With a muffled cry, such as a human being might give, she bent over the kitten licking its wounds and moaning. Suddenly she seemed to realize that it was dead, and again threw her eyes up at us. I shall never forget the sight, for she looked the perfect incarnation of hate. Her green eyes blazed with lurid fire, and the white, sharp teeth seemed to almost shine through the blood which dabbled her mouth and whiskers. She gnashed her teeth, and her claws stood out stark and at full length on every paw. Then she made a wild rush up the wall as if to reach us, but when the momentum ended fell back, and further added to her horrible appearance for she fell on the kitten, and rose with her black fur smeared with its brains and blood. Amelia turned quite faint, and I had to lift her back from the wall. There was a seat close by in shade of a spreading plane tree, and here I placed her while she composed herself. Then I went back to Hutcheson, who stood without moving, looking down on the angry cat below.

As I joined him, he said:

"Wall, I guess that air the savagest beast I ever see—'cept once when an Apache squaw had an edge on a half-breed what they nicknamed 'Splinters' 'cos of the way he fixed up her papoose which he stole on a raid just to show that he appreciated the way they had given his mother the fire torture. She

She looked the perfect incarnation of hate.

got that kinder look so set on her face that it jest seemed to grow there. She followed Splinters mor'n three year till at last the braves got him and handed him over to her. They did say that no man, white or Injun, had ever been so long a-dying under the tortures of the Apaches. The only time I ever see her smile was when I wiped her out. I kem on the camp just in time to see Splinters pass in his checks, and he wasn't sorry to go either. He was a hard citizen, and though I never could shake with him after that papoose business—for it was bitter bad, and he should have been a white man, for he looked like one—I see he had got paid out in full. Durn me, but I took a piece of his hide from one of his skinnin' posts an' had it made into a pocketbook. It's here now!" and he slapped the breast pocket of his coat.

While he was speaking the cat was continuing her frantic efforts to get up the wall. She would take a run back and then charge up, sometimes reaching an incredible height. She did not seem to mind the heavy fall which she got each time but started with renewed vigor; and at every tumble her appearance became more horrible. Hutcheson was a kind-hearted man—my wife and I had both noticed little acts of kindness to animals as well as to persons—and he seemed concerned at the state of fury to which the cat had wrought herself.

"Wall, now!" he said, "I du declare that that poor critter seems quite desperate. There! there! poor thing, it was all an accident—though that won't bring back your little one to you. Say! I wouldn't have had such a thing happen for a thousand! Just shows what a clumsy fool of a man can do when he tries to play! Seems I'm too darned slipper-handed to even play with a cat. Say colonel!"—it was a pleasant way he had to bestow titles freely—"I hope your wife don't hold no grudge against me on account of this unpleasantness? Why, I wouldn't have had it occur on no account."

He came over to Amelia and apologized profusely, and she with her usual kindness of heart hastened to assure him that she quite understood that it was an accident. Then we all went again to the wall and looked over.

The cat missing Hutcheson's face had drawn back across the moat, and was sitting on her haunches as though ready to spring. Indeed, the very instant she saw him she did spring, and with a blind unreasoning fury, which would have been grotesque, only that it was so frightfully real. She did not try to run up the wall, but simply launched herself at him as though hate and fury could lend her wings to pass straight through the great distance between them. Amelia, womanlike, got quite concerned, and said to Elias P. in a warning voice:

"Oh! you must be very careful. That animal would try to kill you if she were here; her eyes look like positive murder."

He laughed out jovially. "Excuse me, ma'am," he said, "but I can't help laughin'. Fancy a man that has fought grizzlies an' Injuns bein' careful of bein' murdered by a cat!"

When the cat heard him laugh, her whole demeanor seemed to change. She no longer tried to jump or run up the wall, but went quietly over, and sitting again beside the dead kitten began to lick and fondle it as though it were alive.

"See!" said I, "the effect of a really strong man. Even that animal in the midst of her fury recognizes the voice of a master, and bows to him!"

"Like a squaw!" was the only comment of Elias P. Hutcheson, as we moved on our way round the city fosse. Every now and then we looked over the wall and each time saw the cat following us. At first she had kept going back to the dead kitten, and then as the distance grew greater took it in her mouth and so followed. After a while, however, she abandoned this, for we saw her following all alone; she had evidently hidden the body somewhere. Amelia's alarm grew at the cat's persistence, and more than once she repeated her warning; but the American always laughed with amusement, till finally, seeing that she was beginning to be worried, he said:

"I say, ma'am, you needn't be skeered over that cat. I go heeled, I du!" Here he slapped his pistol pocket at the back of his lumbar region. "Why sooner'n have you worried, I'll shoot the critter, right here, an' risk the police interferin' with a citizen of the United States for carryin' arms contrary to reg'lations!" As he spoke he looked over the wall, but the cat on seeing him, retreated, with a growl, into a bed of tall flowers, and was hidden. He went on: "Blest if that ar critter ain't got more sense of what's good for her than most Christians. I guess we've seen the last of her! You bet, she'll go back now to that busted kitten and have a private funeral of it, all to herself!"

Amelia did not like to say more, lest he might, in mistaken kindness to her, fulfill his threat of shooting the cat: and so we went on and crossed the little wooden bridge leading to the gateway whence ran the steep paved roadway between the Burg and the pentagonal Torture Tower. As we crossed the bridge we saw the cat again down below us. When she saw us her fury seemed to return, and she made frantic efforts to get up the steep wall. Hutcheson laughed as he looked down at her, and said:

"Good-by, old girl. Sorry I injured your feelin's, but you'll get over it in time! So long!" And then we passed through the long, dim archway and came to the gate of the Burg.

When we came out again after our survey of this most beautiful old place which not even the well-intentioned efforts of the Gothic restorers of forty years ago have been able to spoil—though their restoration was then glaring white—we seemed to have quite forgotten the unpleasant episode of the morning. The old lime tree with its great trunk gnarled with the passing of nearly nine centuries, the deep well cut through the heart of the rock by those captives of old, and the lovely view from the city wall whence we heard, spread over almost a full quarter of an hour, the multitudinous chimes of the city, had all helped to wipe out from our minds the incident of the slain kitten.

We were the only visitors who had entered the Torture Tower that morning—so at least said the old custodian—and as we had the place all to ourselves were able to make a minute and more satisfactory survey than would have otherwise been possible. The custodian, looking to us as the sole source of his gains for the day, was willing to meet our wishes in any way. The Torture Tower is truly a grim place, even now when many thousands of visitors have sent a stream of life, and the joy that follows life, into the place; but at the time I mention it wore its grimmest and most gruesome aspect. The dust of ages seemed to have settled on it, and the darkness and the horror of its memories seem to have become sentient in a way that would have satisfied the Pantheistic souls of Philo or Spinoza. The lower chamber where we entered was seemingly, in its normal state, filled with incarnate darkness; even the hot sunlight streaming in through the door seemed to be lost in the vast thickness of the walls, and only showed the masonry rough as when the builder's scaffolding had come down, but coated with dust and marked here and there with patches of dark stain which, if walls could speak, could have given their own dread memories of fear and pain. We were glad to pass up the dusty wooden staircase, the custodian leaving the outer door open to light us somewhat on our way; for to our eyes the one long-wick'd, evil-smelling candle stuck in a sconce on the wall gave an inadequate light. When we came up through the open trap in the corner of the chamber overhead, Amelia held on to me so tightly that I could actually feel her heart beat. I must say for my own part that I was not surprised at her fear, for this room was even more gruesome than that below. Here there was certainly more light, but only just sufficient to realize the horrible surroundings of the place. The builders of the tower had evidently intended that only they who should gain the top should have any of the joys of light and prospect. There, as we had noticed from below, were ranges of windows, albeit of medieval smallness, but elsewhere in the tower were only a very few narrow slits such as were habitual in places of medieval defense. A few of these only lit the chamber, and these so high up in the wall that from no part could the sky be seen through the thickness of the walls. In racks, and leaning in disorder against the walls, were a number of headsmen's swords, great double-handed weapons with broad blade and keen edge. Hard by were several blocks whereon the necks of the victims had lain, with here and there deep notches where the steel had bitten through the guard of flesh and shored into the wood. Round the chamber, placed in all sorts of irregular ways, were many implements of torture which made one's heart ache to see—chairs full of spikes which gave instant and excruciating pain; chairs and couches with dull knobs whose torture was seemingly less, but which, though slower, were equally efficacious; racks, belts, boots, gloves, collars, all made for compressing at will; steel baskets in which the head could be slowly crushed into a pulp if necessary; watchmen's hooks with long handle and knife that cut at resistance—this a specialty of the old Nurnberg police system; and many, many other devices for man's injury to man. Amelia grew quite pale with the horror of the things, but fortunately did not faint, for being a little overcome she sat down on a torture chair, but jumped up again with a shriek, all tendency to faint gone. We both pretended that it was the injury done to her dress by the dust of the chair, and the rusty spikes which had upset her, and Mr. Hutcheson acquiesced in accepting the explanation with a kind-hearted laugh.

But the central object in the whole of this chamber of horrors was the engine known as the Iron Virgin, which stood near the center of the room.

It was a rudely shaped figure of a woman, something of the bell order, or, to make a closer comparison, of the figure of Mrs. Noah in the children's Ark, but without that slimness of waist and perfect *rondeur* of hip which marks the aesthetic type of the Noah family. One would hardly have recognized it as intended for a human figure at all had not the founder shaped on the forehead a rude semblance of a woman's face. This machine was coated with rust without, and covered with dust; a rope was fastened to a ring in the front of the figure, about where the waist should have been, and was drawn through a pulley, fastened on the wooden pillar which sustained the flooring above. The custodian pulling this rope showed that a section of the front was hinged like a door at one side; we then saw that the engine was of considerable thickness, leaving just room enough inside for a man to be placed. The door was of equal thickness and of great weight, for it took the custodian all his strength, aided though he was by the contrivance of the pulley, to open it. This weight was partly due to the fact that the door was of manifest purpose hung so as to throw its weight downwards, so that it might shut of its own accord when the strain was released. The inside was honeycombed with rust—nay more, the rust alone that comes through time would hardly have eaten so deep into the iron walls; the rust of the cruel stains was deep indeed! It was only, however, when we came to look at the inside of the door that the diabolical intention was manifest to the full. Here were several long spikes, square and massive, broad at the base and sharp at the points, placed in such a position that when the door should close the upper ones would pierce the eyes of the victim, and the lower ones his heart and vitals. The sight was too much for poor Amelia, and this time she fainted dead off, and I had to carry her down the stairs, and place her on a bench outside till she recovered. That she felt it to the quick was afterwards shown by the fact that my eldest son bears to this day a rude birthmark on his breast, which has, by family consent, been accepted as representing the Nurnberg Virgin.

When we got back to the chamber we found Hutcheson still opposite the Iron Virgin; he had been evidently philosophizing, and now gave us the benefit of his thought in the shape of a sort of exordium.

"Wall, I guess I've been learnin' somethin' here while madam has been gettin' over her faint. 'Pears to me that we're a long way behind the times on our side of the big drink. We uster think out on the plains that the Injun could give us points in tryin' to make a man uncomfortable; but I guess your old medieval law-and-order party could raise him every time. Splinters was pretty good in his bluff on the squaw, but this here young miss held a straight flush all high on him. The points of them spikes air sharp enough still, though even the edges air eaten out by what uster be on them. It'd be a good thing for our Indian section to get some specimens of this here play-toy to send round to the Reservations jest to knock the stuffin' out of the bucks, and the squaws too, by showing them as how old civilization lays over them at their best. Guess but I'll get in that box a minute jest to see how it feels!"

"Oh no! no!" said Amelia. "It is too terrible!"

"Guess, ma'am, nothin's too terrible to the explorin' mind. I've been in some queer places in my time. Spent a night inside a dead horse while a prairie fire swept over me in Montana Territory—an' another time slept inside a dead buffler when the Comanches was on the war path an' I didn't keer to leave my kyard on them. I've been two days in a caved-in tunnel in the Billy Broncho gold mine in New Mexico, an' was one of the four shut up for three parts of a day in the caisson what slid over on her side when we was settin' the foundations of the Buffalo Bridge. I've not funked an odd experience yet, an' I don't propose to begin now!"

We saw that he was set on the experiment, so I said: "Well, hurry up, old man, and get through it quick!"

"All right, general," said he, "but I calculate we ain't quite ready yet. The gentlemen, my predecessors, what stood in that thar canister, didn't volunteer for the office—not much! And I guess there was some ornamental tyin' up before the big stroke was made. I want to go into this thing fair and square, so I must get fixed up proper first. I dare say this old galoot can rise some string and tie me up accordin' to sample?"

This was said interrogatively to the old custodian, but the latter, who understood the drift of his speech, though perhaps not appreciating to the full the niceties of dialect and imagery, shook his head. His protest was, however, only formal and made to be overcome. The American thrust a gold piece into his hand, saying: "Take it, pard! It's your pot; and don't be skeer'd. This ain't no necktie party that you're asked to assist in!" He produced some thin frayed rope and proceeded to bind our companion with sufficient strictness for the purpose. When the upper part of his body was bound, Hutcheson said:

"Hold on a moment, judge. Guess I'm too heavy for you to tote into the canister. You jest let me walk in, and then you can wash up regardin' my legs!"

While speaking he had backed himself into the opening which was just enough to hold him. It was a close fit and no mistake. Amelia looked on with fear in her eyes, but she evidently did not like to say anything. Then the custodian completed his task by tying the American's feet together so that he was now absolutely helpless and fixed in his voluntary prison. He seemed to really enjoy it, and the incipient smile which was habitual to his face blossomed into actuality as he said:

"Guess this here Eve was made out of the rib of a dwarf! There ain't much room for a full-grown citizen of the United States to hustle. We uster make our coffins more roomier in Idaho territory. Now, judge, you jest begin to let this door down, slow, on to me. I want to feel the same pleasure as the other jays had when those spikes began to move toward their eyes!"

"Oh no! no! no!" broke in Amelia hysterically. "It is too terrible! I can't bear to see it!—I can't! I can't!"

But the American was obdurate. "Say, colonel," said he, "why not take madame for a little promenade? I wouldn't hurt her feelin's for the world; but now that I am here, havin' kem eight thousand miles, wouldn't it be too hard to give up the very experience I've been pinin' an' pantin' fur? A man can't get to feel like canned goods every time! Me and the judge here'll fix up this thing in no time, an' then you'll come back, an' we'll all laugh together!"

Once more the resolution that is born of curiosity triumphed, and Amelia stayed holding tight to my arm and shivering while the custodian began to slacken slowly inch by inch the rope that held back the iron door. Hutcheson's face was positively radiant as his eyes followed the first movement of the spikes.

"Wall!" he said, "I guess I've not had enjoyment like this since I left Noo York. Bar a scrap with a French sailor at Wapping—an' that warn't much of a picnic neither—I've not had a show fur real pleasure in this dod-rotted

Continent, where there ain't no b'ars nor no Injuns, an' where nary man goes heeled. Slow there, judge! Don't you rush this business! I want a show for my money this game—I du!"

The custodian must have had in him some of the blood of his predecessors in that ghastly tower, for he worked the engine with a deliberate and excruciating slowness which after five minutes, in which the outer edge of the door had not moved half as many inches, began to overcome Amelia. I saw her lips whiten, and felt her hold upon my arm relax. I looked around an instant for a place whereon to lay her, and when I looked at her again found that her eye had become fixed on the side of the Virgin. Following its direction I saw the black cat crouching out of sight. Her green eyes shone like danger lamps in the gloom of the place, and their color was heightened by the blood which still smeared her coat and reddened her mouth. I cried out:

"The cat! Look out for the cat!" for even then she sprang out before the engine. At this moment she looked like a triumphant demon. Her eyes blazed with ferocity, her hair bristled out till she seemed twice her normal size, and her tail lashed about as does a tiger's when the quarry is before it. Elias P. Hutcheson when he saw her was amused, and his eyes positively sparkled with fun as he said:

"Darned if the squaw hain't got on all her war paint! Jest give her a shove off if she comes any of her tricks on me, for I'm so fixed everlastingly by the boss, that durn my skin if I can keep my eyes from her if she wants them! Easy there, judge! Don't you slack that ar rope or I'm euchered!"

At this moment Amelia completed her faint, and I had to clutch hold of her round the waist or she would have fallen to the floor. While attending to her I saw the black cat crouching for a spring, and jumped up to turn the creature out.

But at that instant, with a sort of hellish scream, she hurled herself, not as we expected at Hutcheson, but straight at the face of the custodian. Her claws seemed to be tearing wildly as one sees in the Chinese drawings of the dragon rampant, and as I looked I saw one of them light on the poor man's eye, and actually tear through it and down his cheek, leaving a wide band of red where the blood seemed to spurt from every vein.

With a yell of sheer terror which came quicker than even his sense of pain, the man leaped back, dropping as he did so the rope which held back the iron door. I jumped for it, but was too late, for the cord ran like lightning through the pulley block, and the heavy mass fell forward from its own weight.

As the door closed I caught a glimpse of our poor companion's face. He seemed frozen with terror. His eyes stared with a horrible anguish as if dazed, and no sound came from his lips.

And then the spikes did their work. Happily the end was quick, for when I wrenched open the door they had pierced so deep that they had locked in the bones of the skull through which they had crushed, and actually tore him—it—out of his iron prison till, bound as he was, he fell at full length with a sickly thud upon the floor, the face turning upward as he fell.

I rushed to my wife, lifted her up and carried her out, for I feared for her very reason if she should wake from her faint to such a scene. I laid her on the bench outside and ran back. Leaning against the wooden column was the custodian moaning in pain while he held his reddening handkerchief to his eyes. And sitting on the head of the poor American was the cat, purring loudly as she licked the blood which trickled through the gashed socket of his eyes.

I think no one will call me cruel because I seized one of the old executioner's swords and shore her in two as she sat.

Here There Be Tygers

By Stephen King

Charles needed to go the bathroom very badly.

There was no longer any use in trying to fool himself that he could wait for recess. His bladder was screaming at him, and Miss Bird had caught him squirming.

There were three third-grade teachers in the Acorn Street Grammar School. Miss Kinney was young and blonde and bouncy and had a boyfriend who picked her up after school in a blue Camaro. Mrs. Trask was shaped like a Moorish pillow and did her hair in braids and laughed boomingly. And there was Miss Bird.

Charles had known he would end up with Miss Bird. He had *known* that. It had been inevitable. Because Miss Bird obviously wanted to destroy him. She did not allow children to go to the basement. The basement, Miss Bird said, was where the boilers were kept, and well-groomed ladies and gentlemen would never go down *there,* because basements were nasty, sooty old things. Young ladies and gentlemen do not go to the basement, she said. They go to the *bathroom.*

Charles squirmed again.

Miss Bird cocked an eye at him. "Charles," she said clearly, still pointing her pointer at Bolivia, "do you need to go to the bathroom?"

Cathy Scott in the seat ahead of him giggled, wisely covering her mouth.

Kenny Griffen sniggered and kicked Charles under his desk.

Charles went bright red.

"Speak up, Charles," Miss Bird said brightly. "Do you need to—"

(urinate she'll say urinate she always does)

"Yes, Miss Bird."

"Yes, what?"

"I have to go to the base—to the bathroom."

Miss Bird smiled. "Very well, Charles. You may go to the bathroom and urinate. Is that what you need to do? Urinate?"

Charles hung his head, convicted.

"Very well, Charles. You may do so. And next time kindly don't wait to be asked."

General giggles. Miss Bird rapped the board with her pointer.

Charles trudged up the row towards the door, thirty pairs of eyes boring into his back, and every one of those kids, including Cathy Scott, knew that he was going into the bathroom to urinate. The door was at least a football field's length away. Miss Bird did not go on with the lesson but kept her silence until he had opened the door, entered the blessedly empty hall, and shut the door again.

He walked down towards the boys' bathroom

(basement basement basement IF I WANT)

dragging his fingers along the cool tile of the wall, letting them bounce over the thumbtack-stippled bulletin board and slide lightly across the red

(BREAK GLASS IN CASE OF EMERGENCY)

fire-alarm box.

Miss Bird *liked* it. Miss Bird *liked* making him have a red face. In front of Cathy Scott—who never needed to go to the basement, was that fair?—and everybody else.

Old b-i-t-c-h, he thought. He spelled because he had decided last year God didn't say it was a sin if you spelled.

He went into the boys' bathroom.

It was very cool inside, with a faint, not unpleasant smell of chlorine hanging pungently in the air. Now, in the middle of the morning, it was clean and deserted, peaceful and quite pleasant, not at all like the smoky, stinky cubicle at the Star Theatre downtown.

The bathroom

(!basement!)

was built like an L, the short side lined with tiny square mirrors and white porcelain washbowls and a paper towel dispenser,

(NIBROC)

the longer side with two urinals and three toilet cubicles.

Charles went around the corner after glancing morosely at his thin, rather pallid face in one of the mirrors.

The tiger was lying down at the far end, just underneath the pebbly-white window. It was a large tiger, with tawny Venetian blinds and dark stripes laid across its pelt. It looked up alertly at Charles, and its green eyes narrowed. A kind of silky, purring grunt issued from its mouth. Smooth muscles flexed, and the tiger got to its feet. Its tail switched, making little chinking sounds against the porcelain side of the last urinal.

The tiger looked quite hungry and very vicious.

Charles hurried back the way he had come. The door seemed to take forever to wheeze pneumatically closed behind him, but when it did, he considered himself safe. This door only swung in, and he could not remember ever reading or hearing that tigers are smart enough to open doors.

Charles wiped the back of his hand across his nose. His heart was thumping so hard he could hear it. He still needed to go to the basement, worse than ever.

He squirmed, winced, and pressed a hand against his belly. He *really* had to go to the basement. If he could only be sure no one would come, he could use the girls'. It was right across the hall. Charles looked at it longingly, knowing he would never dare, not in a million years. What if Cathy Scott should come? Or—black horror!—what if *Miss Bird* should come?

Perhaps he had imagined the tiger.

He opened the door wide enough for one eye and peeked in.

The tiger was peeking back from around the angle of the L, its eye a sparkling green. Charles fancied he could see a tiny blue fleck in that deep brilliance, as if the tiger's eye had eaten one of his own. As if—

A hand slid around his neck.

Charles gave a stifled cry and felt his heart and stomach cram up into his throat. For one terrible moment he thought he was going to wet himself.

It was Kenny Griffen, smiling complacently. "Miss Bird sent me after you 'cause you been gone six years. You're in trouble."

"Yeah, but I can't go to the basement," Charles said, feeling faint with the fright Kenny had given him.

"Yer constipated!" Kenny chortled gleefully. "Wait'll I tell *Caaathy!*"

"You better not!" Charles said urgently. "Besides, I'm not. There's a tiger in there."

"What's he doing?" Kenny asked. "Taking a piss?"

"I don't know," Charles said, turning his face to the wall. "I just wish he'd go away." He began to weep.

"Hey," Kenny said, bewildered and a little frightened. "Hey."

"What if I *have* to go? What if I can't help it? Miss Bird'll say—"

"Come on," Kenny said, grabbing his arm in one hand and pushing the door open with the other. "You're making it up."

They were inside before Charles, terrified, could break free and cower back against the door.

"Tiger," Kenny said disgustedly. "Boy, Miss Bird's gonna *kill* you."

"It's around the other side."

Kenny began to walk past the washbowls. "Kitty-kitty-kitty? Kitty?"

"Don't!" Charles hissed.

Kenny disappeared around the corner. "Kitty-kitty? Kitty-kitty? Kit—"

Charles darted out the door again and pressed himself against the wall, waiting, his hands over his mouth and his eyes squinched shut, waiting, waiting for the scream.

There was no scream.

He had no idea how long he stood there, frozen, his bladder bursting. He looked at the door of the boys' basement. It told him nothing. It was just a door.

He wouldn't.

He *couldn't.*

But at last he went in.

The washbowls and the mirrors were neat, and the faint smell of chlorine was unchanged. But there seemed to be a smell under it. A faint, unpleasant smell, like freshly sheared copper.

With groaning (but silent) trepidation, he went to the corner of the L and peeped around.

The tiger was sprawled on the floor, licking its large paws with a long pink tongue. It looked incuriously at Charles. There was a torn piece of shirt caught in one set of claws.

The tiger was sprawled on the floor.

But his need was a white agony now, and he couldn't help it. He *had* to. Charles tiptoed back to the white porcelain basin closest the door.

Miss Bird slammed in just as he was zipping his pants.

"Why, you dirty, filthy little boy," she said almost reflectively.

Charles was keeping a weather eye on the corner. "I'm sorry, Miss Bird . . . the tiger . . . I'm going to clean the sink . . . I'll use soap . . . I swear I will . . ."

"Where's Kenneth?" Miss Bird asked calmly.

"I don't know."

He didn't, really.

"Is he back there?"

"No!" Charles cried.

Miss Bird stalked to the place where the room bent. "Come here, Kenneth. Right this moment."

"Miss Bird—"

But Miss Bird was already around the corner. She meant to pounce. Charles thought Miss Bird was about to find out what pouncing was really all about.

He went out the door again. He got a drink at the drinking fountain. He looked at the American flag hanging over the entrance to the gym. He looked at the bulletin board. Woodsy Owl said GIVE A HOOT, DON'T POLLLUTE. Officer Friendly said NEVER RIDE WITH STRANGERS. Charles read everything twice.

Then he went back to the classroom, walked down his row to his seat with his eyes on the floor, and slid into his seat. It was a quarter to eleven. He took out *Roads to Everywhere* and began to read about Bill at the Rodeo.

Man Overboard!

By Winston Churchill

It was a little after half-past nine when the man fell overboard. The mail steamer was hurrying through the Red Sea in the hope of making up the time which the currents of the Indian Ocean had stolen. The night was clear, though the moon was hidden behind clouds. The warm air was laden with moisture. The still surface of the waters was only broken by the movement of the great ship, from whose quarter the long, slanting undulations struck out, like the feathers from an arrow shaft, and in whose wake the froth and air bubbles churned up by the propeller trailed in a narrowing life to the darkness of the horizon.

There was a concert on board. All the passengers were glad to break the monotony of the voyage, and gathered around the piano in the companion-house. The decks were deserted. The man had been listening to the music and joining in the songs. But the room was hot, and he came out to smoke a cigarette and enjoy a breath of the wind which the speedy passage of the liner created. It was the only wind in the Red Sea that night.

The accommodation-ladder had not been unshipped since leaving Aden, and the man walked out on to the platform, as on to a balcony. He leaned his back against the rail and blew a puff of smoke into the air reflectively. The piano struck up a lively turn, and a voice began to sing the first verse of "The Rowdy Dowdy Boys." The measured pulsations of the screw were a subdued but additional accompaniment. The man knew the song. It had been the rage at all the music halls, when he had started for India seven years before. It reminded him of the brilliant and busy streets he had not seen for so long, but was soon to see again. He was just going to join in the chorus, when the railing, which had been insecurely fastened, gave way suddenly with a snap, and he fell backwards into the warm water of the sea amid a great splash.

For a moment he was physically too much astonished to think. Then he realized that he must shout. He began to do this even before he rose to the surface. He achieved a hoarse, inarticulate, half-choked scream. A startled brain suggested the word "Help!" and he bawled this out lustily and with frantic effort six or seven times without stopping. Then he listened.

> Hi! hi! clear the way
> For the Rowdy Dowdy Boys.

The chorus floated back to him across the smooth water, for the ship had already passed completely by. And as he heard the music a long stab of terror drove through his heart. The possibility that he would not be picked up dawned for the first time on his consciousness. The chorus started again—

> Then—I—say—boys,
> Who's for a jolly spree?
> Rum—tum—tiddley—um,
> Who'll have a drink with me?

"Help! Help! Help!" shrieked the man, in desperate fear.

> Fond of a glass now and then,
> Fond of a row or noise;
> Hi! hi! clear the way
> For the Rowdy Dowdy Boys!

The last words drawled out faint and fainter. The vessel was steaming fast. The beginning of the second verse was confused and broken by the ever-growing distance. The dark outline of the great hull was getting blurred. The stern light dwindled.

Then he set out to swim after it with furious energy, pausing every dozen strokes to shout long wild shouts. The disturbed waters of the sea began to settle again to their rest. The widening undulations became ripples. The aerated confusion of the screw fizzed itself upwards and out. The noise and the sounds of life and music died away.

The liner was but a single fading light on the blackness of the waters and a dark shadow against a paler sky.

At length full realization came to the man, and he stopped swimming. He was alone—abandoned. With the understanding his brain reeled. He began again to swim, only now instead of shouting he prayed—mad, incoherent prayers, the words stumbling into one another.

Suddenly a distant light seemed to flicker and brighten. A surge of joy and hope rushed through his mind. They were going to stop—to turn the ship and come back. And with the hope came gratitude. His prayer was answered. Broken words of thanksgiving rose to his lips. He stopped and stared after the light—his soul in his eyes. As he watched it, it grew gradually but steadily smaller. Then the man knew that his fate was certain. Despair succeeded hope. Gratitude gave place to curses. Beating the water with his arms, he raved impotently. Foul oaths burst from him, as broken as his prayers—and as unheeded.

The fit of passion passed, hurried by increasing fatigue. He became silent—silent as was the sea, for even the ripples were subsiding into the glassy smoothness of the surface. He swam on mechanically along the track of the ship, sobbing quietly to himself, in the misery of fear. And the stern light became a tiny speck, yellower but scarcely bigger than some of the stars, which here and there shone between the clouds.

Nearly twenty minutes passed, and the man's fatigue began to change to exhaustion. The overpowering sense of the inevitable pressed upon him. With the weariness came a strange comfort. He need not swim all the long way to Suez. There was another course. He would die. He would resign his existence since he was thus abandoned. He threw up his hands impulsively and sank. Down, down he went through the warm water. The physical death

He became silent.

took hold of him and he began to drown. The pain of that savage grip recalled his anger. He fought with it furiously. Striking out with arms and legs he sought to get back to the air. It was a hard struggle, but he escaped victorious and gasping to the surface. Despair awaited him. Feebly splashing with his hands he moaned in bitter misery—

"I can't—I must. O God! Let me die."

The moon, then in her third quarter, pushed out from behind the concealing clouds and shed a pale, soft glitter upon the sea. Upright in the water, fifty yards away, was a black triangular object. It was a fin. It approached him slowly.

His last appeal had been heard.

The Lottery

By Shirley Jackson

The morning of June 27th was clear and sunny, with the fresh warmth of a full-summer day; the flowers were blossoming profusely and the grass was richly green. The people of the village began to gather in the square, between the post office and the bank, around ten o'clock; in some towns there were so many people that the lottery took two days and had to be started on June 26th, but in this village, where there were only about three hundred people, the whole lottery took less than two hours, so it could begin at ten o'clock in the morning and still be through in time to allow the villagers to get home for noon dinner.

The children assembled first, of course. School was recently over for the summer, and the feeling of liberty sat uneasily on most of them; they tended to gather together quietly for a while before they broke into boisterous play, and their talk was still of the classroom and the teacher, of books and reprimands. Bobby Martin had already stuffed his pockets full of stones, and the other boys soon followed his example, selecting the smoothest and roundest stones; Bobby and Harry Jones and Dickie Delacroix—the villagers pronounces this name "Dellacroy"—eventually made a great pile of stones in one corner of the square and guarded it against the raids of the other boys. The girls stood aside, talking among themselves, looking over their shoulders at the boys, and the very small children rolled in the dust or clung to the hands of their older brothers or sisters.

Soon the men began to gather, surveying their own children, speaking of planting and rain, tractors and taxes. They stood together, away from the pile of stones in the corner, and their jokes were quiet and they smiled rather than laughed. The women, wearing faded house dresses and sweaters, came shortly after their menfolk. They greeted one another and exchanged bits of gossip as they went to join their husbands. Soon the women, standing by their husbands, began to call to their children, and the children came reluctantly, having to be called four or five times. Bobby Martin ducked under his mother's grasping hand and ran, laughing, back to the pile of stones. His father spoke up sharply, and Bobby came quickly and took his place between his father and his oldest brother.

The lottery was conducted—as were the square dances, the teenage club, the Halloween program—by Mr. Summers, who had time and energy to devote to civic activities. He was a round-faced, jovial man and he ran the coal business, and people were sorry for him, because he had no children and his wife was a scold. When he arrived in the square, carrying the black wooden box, there was a murmur of conversation among the villagers, and he waved and called, "Little late today, folks."

The postmaster, Mr. Graves, followed him, carrying a three-legged stool, and the stool was put in the center of the square and Mr. Summers set the black box down on it. The villagers kept their distance, leaving a space between themselves and the stool, and when Mr. Summers said, "Some of you fellows want to give me a hand?" there was a hesitation before two men, Mr. Martin and his oldest son, Baxter, came forward to hold the box steady on the stool while Mr. Summers stirred up the papers inside it.

The original paraphernalia for the lottery had been lost long ago, and the black box now resting on the stool had been put into use even before Old Man Warner, the oldest man in town, was born. Mr. Summers spoke frequently to the villagers about making a new box, but no one liked to upset even as much tradition as was represented by the black box. There was a story that the present box had been made with some pieces of the box that had preceded it, the one that had been constructed when the first people settled down to make a village here. Every year, after the lottery, Mr. Summers began talking again about a new box, but every year the subject was allowed to fade off without anything's being done. The black box grew shabbier each year; by now it was no longer completely black but splintered badly along one side to show the original wood color, and in some places faded or stained.

Mr. Martin and his oldest son, Baxter, held the black box securely on the stool until Mr. Summers had stirred the papers thoroughly with his hand. Because so much of the ritual had been forgotten or discarded, Mr. Summers had been successful in having slips of paper substituted for the chips of wood that had been used for generations. Chips of wood, Mr. Summers had argued, had been all very well when the village was tiny, but now that the population was more than three hundred and likely to keep on growing, it was necessary to use something that would fit more easily into the black box. The night before the lottery, Mr. Summers and Mr. Graves made up the slips of paper and put them in the box, and it was then taken to the safe of Mr. Summers' coal company and locked up until Mr. Summers was ready to take it to the square next morning. The rest of the year, the box was put away, sometimes one place, sometimes another; it had spent one year in Mr. Graves's barn and another year underfoot in the post office, and sometimes it was set on a shelf in the Martin grocery and left there.

There was a great deal of fussing to be done before Mr. Summers declared the lottery open. There were the lists to make up—of heads of families, heads of households in each family, members of each household in each family. There was the proper swearing-in of Mr. Summers by the postmaster, as the official of the lottery; at one time, some people remembered, there had been a recital of some sort, performed by the official of the lottery, a perfunctory, tuneless chant that had been rattled off duly each year; some people believed that the official of the lottery used to stand just so when he said or sang it, others believed that he was supposed to walk among the people, but years and years ago this part of the ritual had been allowed to lapse. There had been, also, a ritual salute, which the official of the lottery had had to use in addressing each person who came up to draw from the box, but this also had changed with time, until now it was felt necessary only for the official to speak to each person approaching. Mr. Summers was very good at all this; in his clean white shirt and blue jeans, with one hand resting carelessly on the black box, he seemed very proper and important as he talked interminably to Mr. Graves and the Martins.

Just as Mr. Summers finally left off talking and turned to the assembled villagers, Mrs. Hutchinson came hurriedly along the path to the square, her sweater thrown over her shoulders, and slid into place in the back of the crowd. "Clean forgot what day it was," she said to Mrs. Delacroix, who stood next to her, and they both laughed softly. "Thought my old man was out back stacking wood," Mrs. Hutchinson went on, "and then I looked out the window and the kids was gone, and then I remembered it was the twenty-seventh and came a-running." She dried her hands on her apron, and Mrs. Delacroix said, "You're in time, though. They're still talking away up there."

Mrs. Hutchinson craned her neck to see through the crowd and found her husband and children standing near the front. She tapped Mrs. Delacroix on the arm as a farewell and began to make her way through the crowd. The people separated good-humoredly to let her through; two or three people said, in voices just loud enough to be heard across the crowd, "Here comes your Missus, Hutchinson," and "Bill, she made it after all." Mrs. Hutchinson reached her husband, and Mr. Summers, who had been waiting, said cheerfully, "Thought we were going to have to get on without you, Tessie." Mrs. Hutchinson said, grinning, "Wouldn't have me leave m'dishes in the sink, now, would you, Joe?" and soft laughter ran through the crowd as the people stirred back into position after Mrs. Hutchinson's arrival.

"Well, now," Mr. Summers said soberly, "guess we better get started, get this over with, so's we can go back to work. Anybody ain't here?"

"Dunbar," several people said. "Dunbar, Dunbar."

Mr. Summers consulted his list. "Clyde Dunbar," he said. "That's right. He's broke his leg, hasn't he? Who's drawing for him?"

"Me, I guess," a woman said, and Mr. Summers turned to look at her. "Wife draws for her husband," Mr. Summers said. "Don't you have a grown boy to do it for you, Janey?" Although Mr. Summers and everyone else in the village knew the answer perfectly well, it was the business of the official of the lottery to ask such questions formally. Mr. Summers waited with an expression of polite interest while Mrs. Dunbar answered.

"Horace's not but sixteen yet," Mrs. Dunbar said regretfully. "Guess I gotta fill in for the old man this year."

"Right," Mr. Summers said. He made a note on the list he was holding. Then he asked, "Watson boy drawing this year?"

A tall boy in the crowd raised his hand. "Here," he said. "I'm drawing for m'mother and me." He blinked his eyes nervously and ducked his head as several voices in the crowd said thing like "Good fellow, Jack," and "Glad to see your mother's got a man to do it."

"Well," Mr. Summers said, "guess that's everyone. Old Man Warner make it?"

"Here," a voice said, and Mr. Summers nodded.

—

A sudden hush fell on the crowd as Mr. Summers cleared his throat and looked at the list. "All ready?" he called. "Now, I'll read the names—heads of families first—and the men come up and take a paper out of the box. Keep the paper folded in your hand without looking at it until everyone has had a turn. Everything clear?"

The people had done it so many times that they only half listened to the directions; most of them were quiet, wetting their lips, not looking around. Then Mr. Summers raised one hand high and said, "Adams." A man disengaged himself from the crowd and came forward. "Hi, Steve," Mr. Summers said, and Mr. Adams said, "Hi, Joe." They grinned at one another humorlessly and nervously. Then Mr. Adams reached into the black box and took out a folded paper. He held it firmly by one corner as he turned and went hastily back to his place in the crowd, where he stood a little apart from his family, not looking down at his hand.

"Allen," Mr. Summers said. "Anderson . . . Bentham."

"Seems like there's no time at all between lotteries any more," Mrs. Delacroix said to Mrs. Graves in the back row. "Seems like we got through with the last one only last week."

"Time sure goes fast," Mrs. Graves said.

"Clark . . . Delacroix."

"There goes my old man," Mrs. Delacroix said. She held her breath while her husband went forward.

"Dunbar," Mr. Summers said, and Mrs. Dunbar went steadily to the box while one of the women said, "Go on, Janey," and another said, "There she goes."

"We're next," Mrs. Graves said. She watched while Mr. Graves came around from the side of the box, greeted Mr. Summers gravely, and selected a slip of paper from the box. By now, all through the crowd there were men holding the small folded papers in their large hands, turning them over and over nervously. Mrs. Dunbar and her two sons stood together, Mrs. Dunbar holding the slip of paper.

A sudden hush fell on the crowd.

"Harburt . . . Hutchinson."

"Get up there, Bill," Mrs. Hutchinson said, and the people near her laughed.

"Jones."

"They do say," Mr. Adams said to Old Man Warner, who stood next to him, "that over in the north village they're talking of giving up the lottery."

Old Man Warner snorted. "Pack of crazy fools," he said. "Listening to the young folks, nothing's good enough for *them.* Next thing you know, they'll be wanting to go back to living in caves, nobody work any more, live *that* way for a while. Used to be a saying about 'Lottery in June, corn be heavy soon.' First thing you know, we'd all be eating stewed chickweed and acorns. There's *always* been a lottery," he added petulantly. "Bad enough to see young Joe Summers up there joking with everybody."

"Some places have already quit lotteries," Mrs. Adams said.

"Nothing but trouble in *that,*" Old Man Warner said stoutly. "Pack of young fools."

"Martin." And Bobby Martin watched his father go forward. "Overdyke . . . Percy."

"I wish they'd hurry," Mrs. Dunbar said to her older son. "I wish they'd hurry."

"They're almost through," her son said.

"You get ready to run tell Dad," Mrs. Dunbar said.

Mr. Summers called his own name and then stepped forward precisely and selected a slip from the box. Then he called, "Warner."

"Seventy-seventh year I been in the lottery," Old Man Warner said as he went through the crowd. "Seventy-seventh time."

"Watson." The tall boy came awkwardly through the crowd. Someone said, "Don't be nervous, Jack," and Mr. Summers said, "Take your time, son."

"Zanini."

After that, there was a long pause, a breathless pause, until Mr. Summers, holding his slip of paper in the air, said, "All right, fellows." For a minute, no one moved, and then all the slips of paper were opened. Suddenly, all the women began to speak at once, saying, "Who is it?," "Who's got it?," "Is it the Dunbars?," "Is it the Watsons?" Then the voices began to say, "It's Hutchinson. It's Bill," "Bill Hutchinson's got it."

"Go tell your father," Mrs. Dunbar said to her older son.

People began to look around to see the Hutchinsons. Bill Hutchinson was standing quiet, staring down at the paper in his hand. Suddenly, Tessie Hutchinson shouted to Mr. Summers, "You didn't give him time enough to take any paper he wanted. I saw you. It wasn't fair!"

"Be a good sport, Tessie," Mrs. Delacroix called, and Mrs. Graves said, "All of us took the same chance."

"Shut up, Tessie," Bill Hutchinson said.

"Well, everyone," Mr. Summers said, "That was done pretty fast, and now we've got to be hurrying a little more to get done in time." He consulted his next list. "Bill," he said, "you draw for the Hutchinson family. You got any other households in the Hutchinsons?"

"There's Don and Eva," Mrs. Hutchinson yelled. "Make *them* take their chance!"

"Daughters draw with their husbands' families, Tessie," Mr. Summers said gently. "You know that as well as anyone else."

"It wasn't *fair*," Tessie said.

"I guess not, Joe," Bill Hutchinson said regretfully. "My daughter draws with her husband's family, that's only fair. And I've got no other family except the kids."

"Then, as far as drawing for families is concerned, it's you," Mr. Summers said in explanation, "and as far as drawing for households is concerned, that's you, too. Right?"

"Right," Bill Hutchinson said.

"How many kids, Bill?" Mr. Summers asked formally.

"Three," Bill Hutchinson said. "There's Bill, Jr., and Nancy, and little Dave. And Tessie and me."

"All right, then," Mr. Summers said. "Harry, you got their tickets back?"

Mr. Graves nodded and held up the slips of paper. "Put them in the box, then," Mr. Summers directed. "Take Bill's and put it in."

"I think we ought to start over," Mrs. Hutchinson said, as quietly as she could. "I tell you it wasn't *fair*. You didn't give him time enough to choose. *Every*body saw that."

Mr. Graves had selected the five slips and put them in the box, and he dropped all the papers but those onto the ground, where the breeze caught them and lifted them off.

"Listen, everybody," Mrs. Hutchinson was saying to the people around her.

"Ready, Bill?" Mr. Summers asked, and Bill Hutchinson, with one quick glance around at his wife and children, nodded.

"Remember," Mr. Summers said, "Take the slips and keep them folded until each person has taken one. Harry, you help little Dave." Mr. Graves took the hand of the little boy, who came willingly with him up to the box. "Take a paper out of the box, Davy," Mr. Summers said. Davy put his hand into the box and laughed. "Take just *one* paper," Mr. Summers said. "Harry, you hold it for him." Mr. Graves took the child's hand and removed the folded paper from the tight fist and held it while little Dave stood next to him and looked up at him wonderingly.

"Nancy next," Mr. Summers said. Nancy was twelve, and her school friends breathed heavily as she went forward, switching her skirt, and took a slip daintily from the box. "Bill, Jr.," Mr. Summers said, and Billy, his face red and his feet over-large, nearly knocked the box over as he got a paper out. "Tessie," Mr. Summers said. She hesitated for a minute, looking around defiantly, and then set her lips and went up to the box. She snatched a paper out and held it behind her.

"Bill," Mr. Summers said, and Bill Hutchinson reached into the box and felt around, bringing his hand out at last with the slip of paper in it

The crowd was quiet. A girl whispered, "I hope it's not Nancy," and the sound of the whisper reached the edges of the crowd.

"It's not the way it used to be," Old Man Warner said clearly. "People ain't the way they used to be."

"All right," Mr. Summers said. "Open the papers. Harry, you open little Dave's."

Mr. Graves opened the slip of paper and there was a general sigh through the crowd as he held it up and everyone could see that it was blank. Nancy and Bill, Jr., opened theirs at the same time, and both beamed and laughed, turning around to the crowd and holding their slips of paper above their heads.

"Tessie," Mr. Summers said. There was a pause, and then Mr. Summers looked at Bill Hutchinson, and Bill unfolded his paper and showed it. It was blank.

"It's Tessie," Mr. Summers said, and his voice was hushed. "Show us her paper, Bill."

Bill Hutchinson went over to his wife and forced the slip of paper out of her hand. It had a black spot on it, the black spot Mr. Summers had made the night before with the heavy pencil in the coal-company office. Bill Hutchinson held it up, and there was a stir in the crowd.

"All right, folks," Mr. Summers said. "Let's finish quickly."

Although the villagers had forgotten the ritual and lost the original black box, they still remembered to use stones. The pile of stones the boys had made earlier was ready; there were stones on the ground with the blowing scraps of paper that had come out of the box. Mrs. Delacroix selected a stone so large she had to pick it up with both hands and turned to Mrs. Dunbar. "Come on," she said. "Hurry up."

Mrs. Dunbar had small stones in both hands, and she said, gasping for breath, "I can't run at all. You'll have to go ahead and I'll catch up with you."

The children had stones already, and someone gave little Davy Hutchinson a few pebbles.

Tessie Hutchinson was in the center of a cleared space by now, and she held her hands out desperately as the villagers moved in on her. "It isn't fair," she said. A stone hit her on the side of the head.

Old Man Warner was saying, "Come on, come on, everyone." Steve Adams was in the front of the crowd of villagers, with Mrs. Graves beside him.

"It isn't fair, it isn't right," Mrs. Hutchinson screamed, and then they were upon her.

The Bus-Conductor

By E. F. Benson

My friend, Hugh Grainger, and I had just returned from a two days' visit in the country, where we had been staying in a house of sinister repute which was supposed to be haunted by ghosts of a peculiarly fearsome and truculent sort. The house itself was all that such a house should be, Jacobean and oak-paneled, with long dark passages and high vaulted rooms. It stood, also, very remote, and was encompassed by a wood of somber pines that muttered and whispered in the dark, and all the time that we were there a southwesterly gale with torrents of scolding rain had prevailed, so that by day and night weird voices moaned and fluted in the chimneys, a company of uneasy spirits held colloquy among the trees, and sudden tattoos and tappings beckoned from the window panes. But in spite of these surroundings, which were sufficient in themselves, one would almost say, to spontaneously generate occult phenomena, nothing of any description had occurred. I am bound to add, also, that my own state of mind was peculiarly well adapted to receive or even to invent the sights and sounds we had gone to seek, for I was, I confess, during the whole time that we were there, in a state of abject apprehension, and lay awake both nights through hours of terrified unrest, afraid of the dark, yet more afraid of what a lighted candle might show me.

Hugh Grainger, on the evening after our return to town, had dined with me, and after dinner our conversation, as was natural, soon came back to these entrancing topics.

"But why you go ghost-seeking I cannot imagine," he said, "because your teeth were chattering and your eyes starting out of your head all the time you were there, from sheer fright. Or do you like being frightened?"

Hugh, though generally intelligent, is dense in certain ways; this is one of them.

"Why, of course, I like being frightened," I said. "I want to be made to creep and creep and creep. Fear is the most absorbing and luxurious of emotions. One forgets all else if one is afraid."

"Well, the fact that neither of us saw anything," he said, "confirms what I have always believed."

"And what have you always believed?"

"That these phenomena are purely objective, not subjective, and that one's state of mind has nothing to do with the perception that perceives them, nor have circumstances or surroundings anything to do with them either. Look at Osburton. It has had the reputation of being a haunted house for years, and it certainly has all the accessories of one. Look at yourself, too, with all your nerves on edge, afraid to look round or light a candle for fear of seeing something! Surely there was the right man in the right place then, if ghosts are subjective."

He got up and lit a cigarette, and looking at him—Hugh is about six feet high, and as broad as he is long—I felt a retort on my lips, for I could not help my mind going back to a certain period in his life, when, from some cause which, as far as I knew, he had never told anybody, he had become a mere quivering mass of disordered nerves. Oddly enough, at the same moment and for the first time, he began to speak of it himself.

"You may reply that it was not worth my while to go either," he said, "because I was so clearly the wrong man in the wrong place. But I wasn't. You for all your apprehensions and expectancy have never seen a ghost. But I have, though I am the last person in the world you would have thought likely to do so, and, though my nerves are steady enough again now, it knocked me all to bits."

He sat down again in his chair.

"No doubt you remember my going to bits," he said, "and since I believe that I am sound again now, I should rather like to tell you about it. But before I couldn't; I couldn't speak of it at all to anybody. Yet there ought to have been nothing frightening about it; what I saw was certainly a most useful and friendly ghost. But it came from the shaded side of things; it looked suddenly out of the night and the mystery with which life is surrounded.

"I want first to tell you quite shortly my theory about ghost-seeing," he continued, "and I can explain it best by a simile, an image. Imagine then that you and I and everybody in the world are like people whose eye is directly opposite a little tiny hole in a sheet of cardboard which is continually shifting and revolving and moving about. Back to back with that sheet of cardboard is another, which also, by laws of its own, is in perpetual but independent motion. In it too there is another hole, and when, fortuitously it would seem, these two holes, the one through which we are always looking, and the other in the spiritual plane, come opposite one another, we see through, and then only do the sights and sounds of the spiritual world become visible or audible to us. With most people these holes never come opposite each other during their life. But at the hour of death they do, and then they remain stationary. That, I fancy, is how we 'pass over.'

"Now, in some natures, these holes are comparatively large, and are constantly coming into opposition. Clairvoyants, mediums are like that. But, as far as I knew, I had no clairvoyant or mediumistic powers at all. I therefore am the sort of person who long ago made up his mind that he never would see a ghost. It was, so to speak, an incalculable chance that my minute spy-hole should come into opposition with the other. But it did: and it knocked me out of time."

I had heard some such theory before, and though Hugh put it rather picturesquely, there was nothing in the least convincing or practical about it. It might be so, or again it might not.

"I hope your ghost was more original than your theory," said I, in order to bring him to the point.

"Yes, I think it was. You shall judge."

I put on more coal and poked up the fire. Hugh has got, so I have always considered, a great talent for telling stories, and that sense of drama which is so necessary for the narrator. Indeed, before now, I have suggested to him that he should take this up as a profession, sit by the fountain in Piccadilly

Circus, when times are, as usual, bad, and tell stories to the passers-by in the street, Arabian fashion, for reward. The most part of mankind, I am aware, do not like long stories, but to the few, among whom I number myself, who really like to listen to lengthy accounts of experiences, Hugh is an ideal narrator. I do not care for his theories, or for his similes, but when it comes to facts, to things that happened, I like him to be lengthy.

"Go on, please, and slowly," I said. "Brevity may be the soul of wit, but it is the ruin of story-telling. I want to hear when and where and how it all was, and what you had for lunch and where you had dined and what—"

Hugh began:

"It was the 24th of June, just eighteen months ago," he said. "I had let my flat, you may remember, and came up from the country to stay with you for a week. We had dined alone here—"

I could not help interrupting.

"Did you see the ghost here?" I asked. "In this square little box of a house in a modern street?"

"I was in the house when I saw it."

I hugged myself in silence.

"We had dined alone here in Graeme Street," he said, "and after dinner I went out to some party, and you stopped at home. At dinner your man did not wait, and when I asked where he was, you told me he was ill, and, I thought, changed the subject rather abruptly. You gave me your latch-key when I went out, and on coming back, I found you had gone to bed. There were, however, several letters for me, which required answers. I wrote them there and then, and posted them at the pillar-box opposite. So I suppose it was rather late when I went upstairs.

"You had put me in the front room, on the third floor, overlooking the street, a room which I thought you generally occupied yourself. It was a very hot night, and though there had been a moon when I started to my party, on my return the whole sky was cloud-covered, and it both looked and felt as if we might have a thunderstorm before morning. I was feeling very sleepy and heavy, and it was not till after I had got into bed that I noticed by the shadows of the window-frames on the blind that only one of the windows was open. But it did not seem worth while to get out of bed in order to open it, though I felt rather airless and uncomfortable, and I went to sleep.

"What time it was when I awoke I do not know, but it was certainly not yet dawn, and I never remember being conscious of such an extraordinary stillness as prevailed. There was no sound either of foot-passengers or wheeled traffic; the music of life appeared to be absolutely mute. But now instead of being sleepy and heavy, I felt, though I must have slept an hour or two at most, since it was not yet dawn, perfectly fresh and wide-awake, and the effort which had seemed not worth making before, that of getting out of bed and opening the other window, was quite easy now and I pulled up the blind, threw it wide open, and leaned out, for somehow I parched and pined for air. Even outside the oppression was very noticeable, and though, as you know, I am not easily given to feel the mental effects of climate, I was aware of an awful creepiness coming over me. I tried to analyze it away, but without success; the past day had been pleasant, I looked forward to another pleasant day tomorrow, and yet I was full of some nameless apprehension. I felt, too, dreadfully lonely in this stillness before the dawn.

"Then I heard suddenly and not very far away the sound of some approaching vehicle; I could distinguish the tread of two horses walking at a slow foot's pace. They were, though not yet visible, coming up the street, and yet this indication of life did not abate that dreadful sense of loneliness which I have spoken of. Also in some dim unformulated way that which was coming seemed to me to have something to do with the cause of my apprehension.

"Then the vehicle came into sight. At first I could not distinguish what it was. Then I saw that the horses were black and had long tails, and that what they dragged was made of glass, but had a black frame. It was a hearse. Empty.

"It was moving up this side of the street. It stopped at your door.

"Then the obvious solution struck me. You had said at dinner that your man was ill, and you were, I thought, unwilling to speak more about his illness. No doubt, so I imagined now, he was dead, and for some reason, perhaps because you did not want me to know anything about it, you were having the body removed at night. This, I must tell you, passed through my mind quite instantaneously, and it did not occur to me how unlikely it really was, before the next thing happened.

"I was still leaning out of the window, and I remember also wondering, yet only momentarily, how odd it was that I saw things—or rather the one thing I was looking at—so very distinctly. Of course, there was a moon behind the clouds, but it was curious how every detail of the hearse and the horses was visible. There was only one man, the driver, with it, and the street was otherwise absolutely empty. It was at him I was looking now. I could see every detail of his clothes, but from where I was, so high above him, I could not see his face. He had on gray trousers, brown boots, a black coat buttoned all the way up, and a straw hat. Over his shoulder there was a strap, which seemed to support some sort of little bag. He looked exactly like—well, from my description what did he look exactly like?"

"Why—a bus-conductor," I said instantly.

"So I thought, and even while I was thinking this, he looked up at me. He had a rather long thin face, and on his left cheek there was a mole with a growth of dark hair on it. All this was as distinct as if it had been noonday, and as if I was within a yard of him. But—so instantaneous was all that takes so long in the telling—I had not time to think it strange that the driver of a hearse should be so unfunereally dressed.

"Then he touched his hat to me, and jerked his thumb over his shoulder.

"'Just room for one inside, sir,' he said.

"There was something so odious, so coarse, so unfeeling about this that I instantly drew my head in, pulled the blind down again, and then, for what reason I do not know, turned on the electric light in order to see what time it was. The hands of my watch pointed to half-past eleven.

"It was then for the first time, I think, that a doubt crossed my mind as to the nature of what I had just seen. But I put out the light again, got into bed, and began to think. We had dined; I had gone to a party, I had come back and written letters, had gone to bed and had slept. So how could it be half-past eleven? . . . Or—*what* half-past eleven was it?

"Then another easy solution struck me; my watch must have stopped. But it had not; I could hear it ticking.

"There was stillness and silence again. I expected every moment to hear muffled footsteps on the stairs, footsteps moving slowly and smally under the weight of a heavy burden, but from inside the house there was no sound

The ghastly gaiety of the face.

whatever. Outside, too, there was the same dead silence, while the hearse waited at the door. And the minutes ticked on and ticked on, and at length I began to see a difference in the light in the room, and knew that the dawn was beginning to break outside. But how had it happened, then, that if the corpse was to be removed at night it had not gone, and that the hearse still waited, when morning was already coming?

"Presently I got out of bed again, and with the sense of strong physical shrinking I went to the window and pulled back the blind. The dawn was coming fast; the whole street was lit by that silver hueless light of morning. But there was no hearse there.

"Once again I looked at my watch. It was just a quarter-past four. But I would swear that not half an hour had passed since it had told me that it was half-past eleven.

"Then a curious double sense, as if I was living in the present and at the same moment had been living in some other time, came over me. It was dawn on June 25th, and the street, as natural, was empty. But a little while ago the driver of a hearse had spoken to me, and it was half-past eleven. What was that driver, to what plane did he belong? And again *what* half-past eleven was it that I had seen recorded on the dial of my watch?

"And then I told myself that the whole thing had been a dream. But if you ask me whether I believed what I told myself, I must confess that I did not.

"Your man did not appear at breakfast next morning, nor did I see him again before I left that afternoon. I think if I had, I should have told you about all this, but it was still possible, you see, that what I had seen was a real hearse, driven by a real driver, for all the ghastly gaiety of the face that had looked up to mine, and the levity of his pointing hand. I might possibly have fallen asleep soon after seeing him, and slumbered through the removal of the body and the departure of the hearse. So I did not speak of it to you."

There was something wonderfully straightforward and prosaic in all this; here were no Jacobean houses oak-paneled and surrounded by weeping pine-trees, and somehow the very absence of suitable surroundings made the story more impressive. But for a moment a doubt assailed me.

"Don't tell me it was all a dream," I said.

"I don't know whether it was or not. I can only say that I believe myself to have been wide awake. In any case the rest of the story is—odd.

"I went out of town again that afternoon," he continued, "and I may say that I don't think that even for a moment did I get the haunting sense of what I had seen or dreamed that night out of my mind. It was present to me always as some vision unfulfilled. It was as if some clock had struck the four quarters, and I was still waiting to hear what the hour would be.

"Exactly a month afterwards I was in London again, but only for the day. I arrived at Victoria about eleven, and took the underground to Sloane Square in order to see if you were in town and would give me lunch. It was a baking hot morning, and I intended to take a bus from the King's Road as far as Graeme Street. There was one standing at the corner just as I came out of the station, but I saw that the top was full, and the inside appeared to be full also. Just as I came up to it the conductor, who, I suppose, had been inside, collecting fares or what not, came out on to the step within a few feet of me. He wore gray trousers, brown boots, a black coat buttoned, a straw hat, and over his shoulder was a strap on which hung his little machine for punching tickets. I saw his face, too; it was the face of the driver of the hearse, with a mole on the left cheek. Then he spoke to me, jerking his thumb over his shoulder.

"'Just room for one inside, sir,' he said.

"At that a sort of panic-terror took possession of me, and I knew I gesticulated wildly with my arms, and cried, 'No, no!' But at that moment I was living not in the hour that was then passing, but in that hour which had passed a month ago, when I leaned from the window of your bedroom here just before the dawn broke. At this moment too I knew that my spy-hole had been opposite the spy-hole into the spiritual world. What I had seen there had some significance, now being fulfilled, beyond the significance of the trivial happenings of today and tomorrow. The Powers of which we know so little were visibly working before me. And I stood there on the pavement shaking and trembling.

"I was opposite the post-office at the corner, and just as the bus started my eye fell on the clock in the window there. I need not tell you what the time was.

"Perhaps I need not tell you the rest, for you probably conjecture it, since you will not have forgotten what happened at the corner of Sloane Square at the end of July, the summer before last. The bus pulled out from the pavement into the street in order to get round a van that was standing in front of it. At the moment there came down the King's Road a big motor going at a hideously dangerous pace. It crashed full into the bus, burrowing into it as a gimlet burrows into a board."

He paused.

"And that's my story," he said.

Thanksgiving

By Joyce Carol Oates

Father spoke quietly. "We'll do the shopping for your mother, the turkey and all. You know she isn't feeling well."

At once I asked, "What's wrong with her?"

I thought I knew. Probably. It had been three days now. But the question was what any father would have expected of any daughter of thirteen.

My voice, too, was a thirteen-year-old's. A scrawny sort of voice, drawling, skeptical.

Father seemed not to hear. Hitched up his trousers, rattled the keys to the pick-up as a man does who likes the feel of keys, the noisy rattle. "We'll just do it. We'll surprise her. Then it will be done." He counted on his fingers, smiling. "Thanksgiving is on Thursday, day after tomorrow. We'll surprise her so she can get started early." Yet there was a vagueness in his pebble-colored eyes, that moved upon me scarcely seeing me; as if, standing before him, a long-legged skinny girl all elbows and knees and pimples gritty as sand scattered across her forehead, I was no more to him than the horizon of scrub pine a short distance away or the weatherworn fake-beige-brick asphalt siding on our house.

Father nodded, grim and pleased. "Yes. She'll see."

With a sigh he climbed up into the truck on the driver's side, and I climbed up into the truck on the passenger's side. It was just getting dark when he turned on the ignition. You needed to make a quick escape from our place, before the dogs rushed out yammering to be taken along—and sure enough, hearing us slam the truck doors, there came running Foxy, Tiki,

Buck, hounds with some terrier blood in them, barking and whining after us. Foxy was my favorite, the one who loved me best, hardly more than a year old but long-bodied and showing her ribs, big wet staring eyes like I'd broken her heart going away without her, but what the hell, you have to go to school without the damn dogs and sometimes to church and sure enough you want to go to town without people smiling at you behind your back, figuring you as a country hick with dogs trailing after. "Go on back!" I yelled at the dogs, but they only yipped and fussed louder, running right alongside the pick-up as Father took it out the drive tossing up gravel in our wake. What a racket! I hoped Mother would not hear.

I was feeling guilty, seeing Foxy left behind, so I poked Father, and asked, "Why don't we take them along, in the back?" and Father said, in a voice like he was talking to some fool, "We're going grocery shopping for your mother, where's your sense?"

Now we were out on the road, and Father had the gas pedal pressed down flat. The fenders of the old truck rattled. That weird high vibration started in the dashboard like a cricket none of us could ever find to stop it.

For the longest time, the dogs ran after us, Buck in the lead, and Foxy second. Long ears flapping, tongues out, like it was warm weather and not an almost-freezing November day. A strange feeling came over me, hearing the dogs barking like that—loud and anxious as they'd bark if they thought we were never coming back. Like I wanted to laugh, but to cry too. Like when you're tickled so hard it begins to hurt and whoever's doing it, tickling you, doesn't know the difference.

Not that I was tickled any more, that old. I don't guess I'd been tickled in years.

The dogs fell farther and farther behind, till I couldn't see them any more in the rearview mirror. Their barking faded too. Still, Father was driving hard. The damn road was so rutted, my teeth rattled in my head. I knew better, though, than to tell Father to slow down, or even to switch on his headlights. (Which he did anyway, a few minutes later.) There was a mix of smells about him—tobacco and beer and that harsh-smelling steel-gray soap he used to get the worst of the grease off his hands. And another smell too, I couldn't name.

Father was saying, like I'd been arguing with him, "Your mother is a good woman. She'll pull out of this."

I didn't like that kind of talk. The age I was, you don't want to hear adults talk about other adults to you. So I made some kind of low, impatient mumble. Not that Father heard, anyway—he wasn't listening.

It was eleven miles to town and once we got on the paved highway Father kept the speedometer needle right at sixty miles per hour. Still, it seemed to take us a long time. Why would it take such a long time? I'd come out without my jacket, just wearing jeans and a plaid wool shirt, and boots; so I was shivering. The sky was on fire, behind the foothills and the mountains in the west. We had to drive over the long shaky bridge across the Yewville River that used to scare me so when I was little, I'd shut my eyes tight until we were on solid land. Except now I wouldn't let myself shut my eyes, I was too old for such cowardice.

I think I knew that something was going to happen. In town, maybe. Or when we returned home.

Father drove straight down the middle of the high wrought-iron vibrating old bridge. Lucky no one was coming in the left lane. I could hear him mumbling to himself, like thinking aloud. "—coupons? In the drawer? Jesus. Forgot to look." I didn't say a word because it made me mad, either of them talking to themselves in my presence. Like somebody picking his nose and not seeing you're there.

(And I knew what Father was talking about too: Mother kept shopping coupons in a kitchen drawer, she'd never go to the A & P without taking a batch of them along in her purse. Claimed she'd saved hundreds of dollars over the years—! What I'd come to think was, grown-up women liked to fuss clipping coupons out of the newspaper ads or shoving their hands up to the elbows in some giant box of detergent or dog chow to fish out a coupon worth twelve cents. You figure it.

For Thanksgiving, though, there'd be a lot of food coupons. "Big savings" on the turkey, plus all the extras. But this year there was nobody in our house to take the time to notice them, let alone cut them out of the ads and file them away.)

Driving to town is driving downhill, mainly. Into the valley. Out of the foothills where it always seemed colder. On the far side of the river, Yewville looked squeezed in, steep streets dropping down to the river, flat-looking, almost vertical, at a distance. I was starting to get that nervous feeling I'd get sometimes when we came to town, and I guessed I wasn't dressed right, or didn't look right—my face, my snarly-frizzy hair. Father made a wrong turn off the bridge ramp before I could stop him so we had to drive through a neighborhood that didn't look familiar: tall narrow row houses built to the sidewalk, some of them boarded-up and empty, and not much traffic on the street; here and there, old rusted tireless hulks of cars at the curbs. There was a thickness to the air as of smoke, and a smell of scorch. All that remained of the fiery sunset was a thin crescent in the west, very far away. The night coming on so fast made me shiver more. And there was the A & P but—what had happened? The smell of smoke and scorch was strong here, you could see that the front of the store was blackened and the plate glass windows that ran the length of it had plywood inserts here and there. The posters advertising special bargains BACON BANANAS TURKEY CRANBERRY MIX EGGS PORTERHOUSE STEAK had begun to peel off the glass and the building itself looked smaller, not as high, as if the roof was sinking in. But there was movement inside. Lights were on, flickering and not very bright, but they were on, and people were inside, shopping.

Father whistled through his teeth, "Well, hell." But pulled into the parking lot. "We'll do it, and get it done." There were only five or six cars in the lot, which looked different from what I remembered—more like raw earth, with weeds growing in cracks, tall thistles. Beyond the parking lot there wasn't anything familiar, no other buildings, or houses, just dark. I whispered, "I don't want to go in there, I'm afraid," but Father already had his door open, so I opened mine too, and jumped down. The smell of smoke and burn was so strong here my nostrils pinched and tears came into my eyes. There was another smell beneath it—wet earth, decomposing matter, garbage.

Grimly, grinning, Father said, "We'll have Thanksgiving like always. Nothing will change that."

—

The automatic doors were not operating, so we had to open the ENTER door by hand, which took some effort. Inside, cold damp air rushed at us—a smell as of the inside of a refrigerator that hadn't been cleaned in a long time. I stifled an impulse to gag. Father sniffed cautiously. "Well, hell!" he murmured again, as if it was a joke. The rear of the store was darkened but there were lighted areas near the front where a few shoppers, most of them women, were pushing carts. Of the eight check-out counters, only two were open. The cashiers were women who looked familiar but they appeared older than I'd remembered, white-lipped and frowning.

"Here we go!" Father said with a broad forced smile, extricating a cart from a snarl of carts. "We'll do this in record time."

One of the cart's wheels stuck every few rotations but Father pushed it hard and impatiently in the direction of the brightest-lit part of the store, which happened to be the fresh produce section, where Mother always shopped first. How it was changed, though!—most of the bins and counters were bare, and some of them were broken; the aisles were partly blocked by mounds of decaying debris and plywood crates. There were puddles on the floor. Flies buzzed groggily. A flush-faced man in a soiled white uniform, a porkpie hat jaunty on his head declaring, in red letters, BARGAIN HOLIDAY BUYS! was snatching heads of lettuce out of a crate and dumping them in a bin so carelessly that some of the heads fell onto the filthy floor at his feet.

Father pushed our cockeyed cart over to this man, and asked him what the hell had happened here, a fire?—but the man just smiled at him without looking at him, a quick angry smile. "No sir!" he said, shaking his head. "Business as usual!"

Rebuffed, Father pushed the cart on. I could see his face reddening.

Of all things, a man hates to be treated rudely by another man in the presence of one of his children.

Father asked me how many people Mother would be cooking for on Thanksgiving, and between us we tried to count. Was it eight? Eleven? Fifteen? I remembered, or thought I remembered, that Mother's older sister was coming this year with her family (husband, five children), but Father said no, they were *not* invited. Father said that Uncle Ryan would be sure to show up, like every year, but I told him no, didn't he remember, Uncle Ryan was dead.

Father blinked, and drew his hand over his stubby jaw, and laughed, his face reddening still more. "Jesus. I guess so."

So we counted, using all our fingers, but couldn't decide. Father said we would have to buy food for the largest number, then, in case they all showed up. Mother would be so upset if something went wrong.

Mother always shopped with a list neatly written in pencil: she'd keep it in plain view in her hand, sending me around the store getting items, up and down the aisles, while she followed more slowly behind, getting the rest, examining prices. It was important to examine prices, she said, because they changed from week to week. Some items were on special, and marked down; others were marked up. But a bargain was not a bargain if it was spoiled or rotten, or just on the brink of being so. Suddenly, with no warning, Father gripped my arm. "Did you bring the list?" he asked. I told him no and he pushed at me, as a child might do. "Why didn't you!" he said.

Father's face in the flickering light was oily, smudged. As if, despite the cold, he was sweating inside his clothes.

"I never saw any list," I said, meanly. "I don't know about any damn list."

We had to get lettuce, though, if Mother was going to make a green salad. We had to get potatoes to be mashed, and yams to be baked, and cranberries for the sauce, and a pumpkin for pie, and apples for applesauce; we had to get carrots, lima beans, celery . . . but the best heads of lettuce I could find were wilted and brown and looked as if insects had been chewing on them. "Put them in the cart, and let's get a move on," Father said, wiping his mouth on his sleeve. "I'll tell her it's the goddamn best we could do." Then he sent me running around, slipping on the wet, puddled floor, trying to find a dozen decent potatoes in a bin of mostly blackened ones, a pumpkin that wasn't soft and beginning to stink, apples that weren't wizened and wormy.

A plump-faced woman with bright orange lipstick and trembling hands was reaching for one of the last good pumpkins but I slipped in under her arm and snatched it away. Open-mouthed, the woman turned to stare at me. Did she know me? Did she know Mother? I pretended not to notice, and hauled the pumpkin to our cart.

The rear of the fresh produce section was blocked off because part of the floor had collapsed, so we had to turn around and retrace our route. Father cursed the grocery cart, which was sticking worse. What else did Mother need? Vinegar, flour, cooking oil, sugar, salt? Bread for the turkey stuffing? I shut my eyes tight trying to envision our kitchen, the inside of the refrigerator that needed cleaning, the cupboard shelves where ants scurried in the dark. They were empty, weren't they, or nearly—it had been many days since Mother had shopped last. But the quavering lights of the A & P were distracting. A sound of dripping close by. And Father speaking to me, his voice loud. "—This aisle? Anything? We need—" His breath was expelled in short steaming pants. He squinted into the semi-darkness where the way was partly blocked by stacks of cartons spilling cans and packages.

I told Father, "I don't want to," and Father told me, "Mother is counting on you girl," and I heard myself sobbing, an angry-ugly sound, "Mother is counting on *you*." But he gave me a nudge and off I went slip-sliding on the floor where water lay in pools two or three inches deep. My breath was steaming, too. I groped quickly for things on the shelves, anything we might need, Mother would want canned applesauce since we wouldn't be bringing her fresh apples, yes and maybe creamed corn, too, maybe canned spinach? beets? pineapple? green beans? And there , on a nearly empty shelf, were cans of tuna fish, bloated and leaking giving off a powerful stink—maybe I should take a few of these, too, for next week? And a big can of Campbell's Pork and Beans: that Father loved.

"Hurry up! What's wrong! We haven't got all night!" Father was calling at me through cupped hands, from the far end of the aisle. I gathered up the canned goods as best I could, hugging them to my chest, but some fell, I had to stoop to pick them up out of the smelly water. "Goddamn you, girl! I said hurry *up!*" I could hear the fear in Father's voice, that I had never heard before.

Shivering, I ran back to Father and dropped the cans in the cart, and we pushed forward.

The next aisle was darkened and partly blocked by loosely strung twine . . . there was a gaping hole in the floor about the size of a full-grown horse. Overhead, part of the ceiling was missing, too: you could look up into the interior of the roof, at the exposed girders. Rust-colored drops of water fell from the girders, heavy as shot. Here were fairly well-stocked shelves of detergent, dish washing soap, toilet cleanser, aerosol insect sprays, ant traps. A woman in a green windbreaker was reaching beyond the blocked-off area to try to get a box of something, teetering on the edge of the hole, but her reach wasn't long enough, she had to give up. I hoped that Father wouldn't make me go down that aisle but, yes, he was pointing, he was determined, "—she'll want soap I guess, for dishes, laundry: go on—" so I knew I hadn't any choice. I slid along sideways as best I could, around the edge of the hole, one foot and then the other, trying to make myself skinnier than I was, not daring to breathe. The rust-colored drops fell in my hair, on my face and hands. *Don't look down. Don't.* I leaned over as far as I could, stretching my arm, my fingers, reaching for a box of detergent. There was regular, economy, giant, jumbo, jumbo-giant: I took the economy because it was closest at hand, and not too heavy. Though it *was* heavy.

I managed to get a box of dish washing soap too, and made my way back to Father who stood leaning against the cart, pressing a hand against his chest where he'd opened his jacket. I was clumsy dropping the detergent into the cart, so it broke, and a fine silvery acid-smelling powder spilled out onto the lettuce. Father cursed me and cuffed me so hard on the side of the head my ear rang and I wondered if my eardrum had broken. Tears flooded into my eyes but I'd be damned if I'd cry.

I wiped my face on my shirt sleeve and whispered, "She doesn't want any of this shit. You know what she wants."

Father slapped me again, on the mouth this time. I rocked back on my heels and tasted blood. "*You're* the little shit," he said, furious.

Father gave the cockeyed cart an angry push, and it lurched forward on three wheels; the fourth wheel was permanently stuck. I wiped my face again and followed after, thinking what choice did I have. Mother *was* counting on me, maybe. If she was counting on anyone at all.

Next was flour, sugar, salt. And next, bakery products: where the shelves were mainly empty, but, on the floor, a few loaves of bread were lying, soggy from the wet. Father grunted in resignation and we picked them up and dropped them in the cart.

Next then was the dairy products section, where a strong smell of spoiled milk and rancid butter prevailed. Father stared at pools of milk underfoot; his mouth worked, but he couldn't speak. I held my nose and plunged in gathering up whatever I could find that wasn't spoiled, or anyway wasn't spoiled too badly. Mother would need milk, yes and cream, yes and butter, and lard. And eggs: we didn't raise chickens any longer, a chicken-flu had carried them all away the previous winter, so we needed eggs, yes but I couldn't find a carton of one dozen eggs that was whole. I squatted on my haunches breathing in little steamy spurts examining eggs, taking a good egg, or anyway what looked like a good egg, from one carton and putting it in another. I wanted at least twelve and this took time and Father was standing a few yards away so nervous waiting I could hear him talking to himself but not his actual words.

I hoped Father was not praying. It would have made me disgusted to hear. The age I was, you don't want to hear any adult, let alone your father, yes and your mother, maybe most of all your mother, praying aloud to God to help them because you know, when you hear such a prayer, there won't be any help.

Next to the dairy products was the frozen food section where it looked as if some giant had smashed things down under his boot. The insides of the refrigerating units were exposed and twisted and gave off an ammonia-like stink. A young mother, fattish, tears on her cheeks, three small children in tow, was searching through mounds of frozen food packages, ice cream packages, while the children fretted and bawled. The cartons of ice cream were mainly melted, flat. The frozen-food dinners must have been thawed. Yet the young mother was stooped over the packages fussing and picking among them, sobbing quietly. I wondered should I look too—we all liked ice cream, and the freezer at home was empty. The ice cream cartons lay in pools of melted ice cream amid something black that seemed to be quivering and seething, like rippling oil. I went to look closer, nudged a quart of raspberry ripple ice cream with my foot, and saw, underneath, a shiny scuttling of cockroaches. The young mother, panting, snatched up a carton of chocolate chip ice cream, shaking off cockroaches, with a sound of disgust; but she put the carton in her shopping cart, along with some others. She looked at me, and smiled, the kind of helpless-angry smile that means, What can you do? I grinned back at her, wiping my sticky hands on my jeans. But I didn't want any of the ice cream, thank you.

Father hissed impatiently, "Come on!" He was shifting his weight from one leg to the other, like he had to go to the bathroom.

So I brought the dairy things back, best as I could, and put them in our cart, which was getting filled at last.

Next, the meat department. Where we had to get our Thanksgiving turkey, if we were going to have a real Thanksgiving. This section, like the frozen foods section, seemed to have been badly damaged. The counters spilled out onto the floor in a mess of twisted metal, broken glass, and spoiling meat—I saw chicken carcasses, coils of sausage like snakes, fat-marbled steaks oozing blood. Here too the smell was overwhelming. Here too roaches were scuttling about. Yet the butcher in his white uniform stood behind the remains of a glass counter, handing over a bloody package of meat to a woman with carrot-red hair and no eyebrows, a high school friend of Mother's whose name I did not know, who made a fool of herself, thanking him so profusely. Father was the next customer, so he stepped up to the counter, asking in a loud voice where was the turkey, and the butcher smirked at him as if he'd asked a fool question, and Father said, louder yet, "Mister, we'd like a good-size bird, twenty pounds at least. My wife—" The butcher was the store's regular butcher, familiar to me, yet changed: a tall, cadaverous man with sunken cheeks, part of his jaw missing, a single beady eye bright with derision. His uniform was filthy with blood and he, too, wore a jaunty porkpie hat with red letters proclaiming BARGAIN HOLIDAY BUYS!

"Turkey's all gone," the butcher said, meanly, with satisfaction, "—except what's left, back in the freezer." He pointed to a wall, beyond a smashed meat counter, where there was a gaping hole; a kind of tunnel. "You want to climb in there and get it, mister, you're welcome to it." Father stared at the hole and worked his mouth but no sound came. I crouched, pinching my nostrils shut with my fingers, and tried to see inside where it was shadowy, and dripping, and there were things (slabs of meat? carcasses?) lying on a glistening floor, and something, or someone, moving.

Father's face was dead-white and his eyes had shrunk in their sockets. He didn't speak, and I didn't speak, but we both knew he couldn't squeeze through a hole that size, even if he tried. Even I would have difficulty.

So I drew a breath, and I said to Father, "Okay. I'll get the damn old turkey." Screwing up my face like a little kid to hide how frightened I was, so he needn't know.

I stepped over some debris and broken glass, got down on my hands and knees—ugh! In that smelly mess!—and poked my head inside the opening. My heart was beating so hard I couldn't get my breath and it scared me to think that I might faint, like Mother. But at the same time I knew I wasn't the kind of girl to faint, I'm strong.

The opening was like a tunnel into a cave, how large the cave was you couldn't see because the edges dissolved out into darkness. The ceiling was

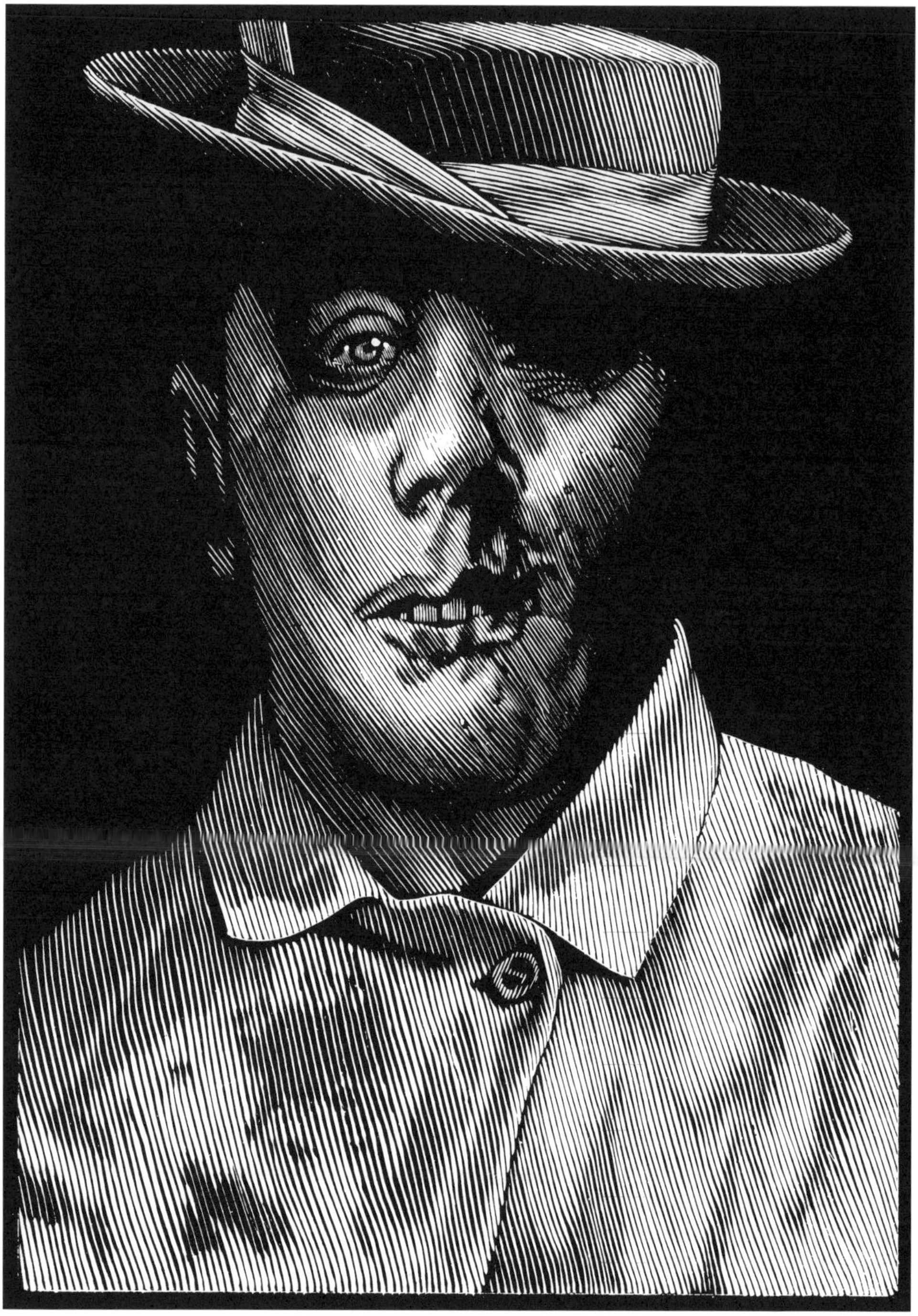

"Turkey's all gone," the butcher said meanly.

low, though, only a few inches above my head. Underfoot were puddles of bloody waste, animal heads, skins, intestines, but also whole sides of beef, parts of a butchered pig, slabs of bacon, blood-stippled turkey carcasses, heads off, necks showing gristle and startlingly white raw bone. I thought that I would vomit, but I managed to control myself. There was one other shopper in here, a woman Mother's age with steely-gray hair in a bun, a good cloth coat with a fur collar and the coat's hem was trailing in the mess but the woman didn't seem to notice. She examined one turkey, rejected it and examined another, rejected that and examined another, finally settling upon a hefty bird which, with a look of grim triumph, she dragged back through the hole. Which left me alone in the cave, shaky, sickish, but excited. I could make out only three or four turkey carcasses remaining. I tried to sniff them wondering were they beginning to go bad? Was one of them still fresh enough to be eaten?—squatting in bloody waste to my ankles. All my life that I could remember up to then, helping Mother in the kitchen, I'd been repulsed by the sight of turkey or chicken carcasses in the sink: the scrawny headless necks, the loose-seeming pale-pimpled skin, the scaly clawy feet. And the smell of them, the unmistakable smell.

Spooning stuffing rich with spices into the bird's scooped-out body, sewing the hole shut, basting with melted fat, roasting. As dead-clammy meat turns to edible meat. As revulsion turns to appetite.

How is it possible you ask, the answer is it *is* possible.

The answer is it *is*.

The smells in the cave were so strong, I couldn't really judge which turkey was fresher than the others so I chose the biggest bird remaining, a twenty-pound bird at least, panting now, half-sobbing with effort I dragged it to the opening, shoved it through, and crawled after it myself. The lights in the store that had seemed dim before now seemed bright, and there was Father standing close by hunched over the grocery cart waiting for me, his mouth agape, a twitchy smile at the corners of his lips. He was so surprised at something, the size of the turkey maybe, or just the fact of it, the fact that I'd done what I'd done, blinking up grinning at him, wiping my filthy hands on my jeans as I stood to my full height, he couldn't even speak at first, and was slow to help me lift the turkey into the cart.

Then weakly, he said, "Well, *hell*."

—

The store was darkening, only one cashier remained to ring up our purchases. Outside, it was very dark; no moon, and a light snow falling, the first snowfall of the year. Father carried the heavier grocery bags, I carried the lighter, to the truck, where we placed them in the rear, and dragged a tarpaulin over them. Father was breathing harshly, his face still unnaturally white, so I wasn't surprised when he told me he wasn't feeling all that good and maybe shouldn't drive home. This was the first time ever I'd been a witness to any adult saying any such thing but somehow I wasn't surprised and when Father gave me the key to the ignition I liked the feel of it in my hand.

We climbed up into the truck. Father in the passenger's seat pressing his fist against his chest; me in the driver's seat, behind the high wheel. I was only just tall enough to see over the wheel and the hood. I'd never driven any vehicle before but I'd watched them, him and her, over the years. So I knew how.

EXCERPT FROM

THE LEGEND OF SLEEPY HOLLOW

By Washington Irving

IT WAS THE VERY witching time of night that Ichabod, heavy-hearted and crestfallen, pursued his travels homewards, along the sides of the lofty hills which rise above Tarry Town, and which he had traversed so cheerily in the afternoon. The hour was as dismal as himself. Far below him the Tappan Zee spread its dusky and indistinct waste of waters, with here and there the tall mast of a sloop, riding quietly at anchor under the land. In the dead hush of midnight, he could even hear the barking of the watchdog from the opposite shore of the Hudson; but it was so vague and faint as only to give an idea of his distance from this faithful companion of man. Now and then, too, the long-drawn crowing of a cock, accidentally awakened, would sound far, far off, from some farmhouse away among the hills—but it was like a dreaming sound in his ear. No signs of life occurred near him, but occasionally the melancholy chirp of a cricket, or perhaps the guttural twang of a bullfrog from a neighboring marsh, as if sleeping uncomfortably and turning suddenly in his bed.

All the stories of ghosts and goblins that he had heard in the afternoon now came crowding upon his recollection. The night grew darker and darker; the stars seemed to sink deeper in the sky, and driving clouds occasionally hid them from his sight. He had never felt so lonely and dismal. He was, moreover, approaching the very place where many of the scenes of the ghost stories had been laid. In the center of the road stood an enormous tulip-tree, which towered like a giant above all the other trees of the neighborhood, and formed a kind of landmark. Its limbs were gnarled and fantastic, large enough to form trunks for ordinary trees, twisting down almost to the earth, and rising again into the air. It was connected with the tragical story of the unfortunate André, who had been taken prisoner hard by; and was universally known by the name of Major André's tree. The common people regarded it with a mixture of respect and superstition, partly out of sympathy for the fate of its ill-starred namesake, and partly from the tales of strange sights, and doleful lamentations, told concerning it.

As Ichabod approached this fearful tree, he began to whistle; he thought his whistle was answered; it was but a blast sweeping sharply through the dry branches. As he approached a little nearer, he thought he saw something white, hanging in the midst of the tree: he paused and ceased whistling but, on looking more narrowly, perceived that it was a place where the tree had been scathed by lightning, and the white wood laid bare. Suddenly he heard a groan—his teeth chattered, and his knees smote against the saddle: it was but the rubbing of one huge bough upon another, as they were swayed about by the breeze. He passed the tree in safety, but new perils lay before him.

About two hundred yards from the tree, a small brook crossed the road, and ran into a marshy and thickly-wooded glen, known by the name of Wiley's Swamp. A few rough logs, laid side by side, served for a bridge over this stream. On that side of the road where the brook entered the wood, a group of oaks and chestnuts, matted thick with wild grape-vines, threw a cavernous gloom over it. To pass this bridge was the severest trial. It was at this identical spot that the unfortunate André was captured, and under the covert of those chestnuts and vines were the sturdy yeomen concealed who surprised him. This has ever since been considered a haunted stream, and fearful are the feelings of the schoolboy who has to pass it alone after dark.

As he approached the stream, his heart began to thump; he summoned up, however, all his resolution, gave his horse half a score of kicks in the ribs, and attempted to dash briskly across the bridge; but instead of starting forward, the perverse old animal made a lateral movement, and ran broadside against the fence. Ichabod, whose fears increased with the delay, jerked the reins on the other side, and kicked lustily with the contrary foot: it was all in vain; his steed started, it is true, but it was only to plunge to the opposite side of the road into a thicket of brambles and alder bushes. The schoolmaster now bestowed both whip and heel upon the starveling ribs of old Gunpowder, who dashed forward, snuffling and snorting, but came to a stand just by the bridge, with a suddenness that had nearly sent his rider sprawling over his head. Just at this moment a plashy tramp by the side of the bridge caught the sensitive ear of Ichabod. In the dark shadow of the grove, on the margin of the brook, he beheld something huge, misshapen and towering. It stirred not, but seemed gathered up in the gloom, like some gigantic monster ready to spring upon the traveler.

The hair of the affrighted pedagogue rose upon his head with terror. What was to be done? To turn and fly was now too late; and besides, what chance was there of escaping ghost or goblin, if such it was, which could ride upon the wings of the wind? Summoning up, therefore, a show of courage, he demanded in stammering accents, "Who are you?" He received no reply. He repeated his demand in a still more agitated voice. Still there was no answer. Once more he cudgeled the sides of the inflexible Gunpowder, and, shutting his eyes, broke forth with involuntary fervor into a psalm tune. Just then the shadowy object of alarm put itself in motion, and with a scramble and a bound stood at once in the middle of the road. Though the night was dark and dismal, yet the form of the unknown might now in some degree be ascertained. He appeared to be a horseman of large dimensions, and mounted on a black horse of powerful frame. He made no offer of molestation or sociability, but kept aloof on one side of the road, jogging along on the blind side of old Gunpowder, who had now got over his fright and waywardness.

Ichabod, who had no relish for this strange midnight companion, and bethought himself of the adventure of Brom Bones with the Galloping Hessian, now quickened his steed in hopes of leaving him behind. The stranger, however, quickened his horse to an equal pace. Ichabod pulled up, and fell into a walk, thinking to lag behind—the other did the same. His heart began to sink within him; he endeavored to resume his psalm tune, but his parched tongue clove to the roof of his mouth, and he could not utter a stave. There was something in the moody and dogged silence of this pertinacious companion that was mysterious and appalling. It was soon fearfully accounted for. On mounting a rising ground, which brought the figure of his fellow-traveler in relief against the sky, gigantic in height, and muffled in a cloak, Ichabod was horror-struck on perceiving that he was headless!—but

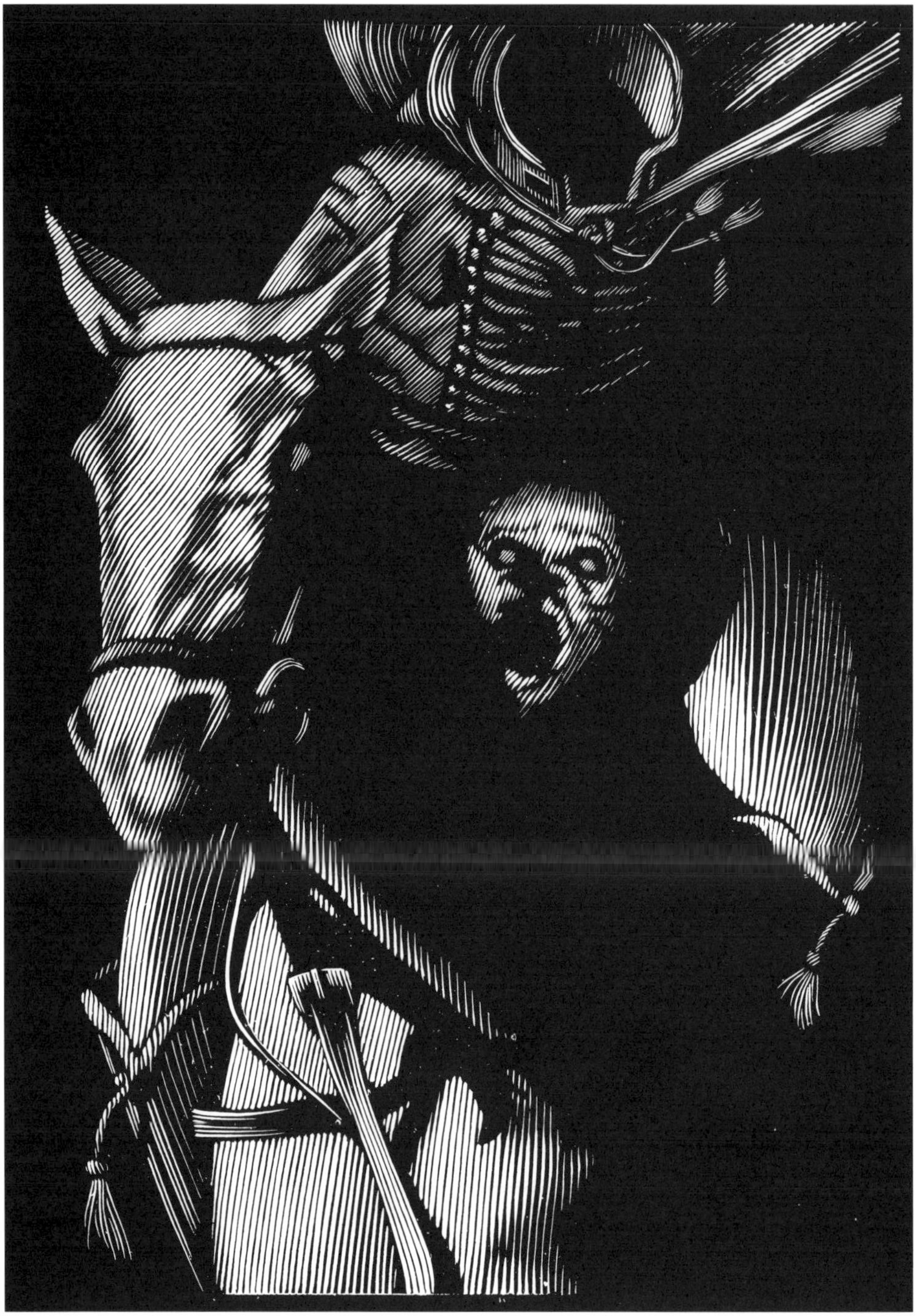

He was headless!

his horror was still more increased on observing that the head, which should have rested on his shoulders, was carried before him on the pommel of his saddle! His terror rose to desperation; he rained a shower of kicks and blows upon Gunpowder, hoping by a sudden movement to give his companion the slip; but the specter started full jump with him. Away, then, they dashed through thick and thin; stones flying and sparks flashing at every bound. Ichabod's flimsy garments fluttered in the air, as he stretched his long lank body away over his horse's head, in the eagerness of his flight.

They had now reached the road which turns off to Sleepy Hollow; but Gunpowder, who seemed possessed with a demon, instead of keeping up it, made an opposite turn, and plunged headlong downhill to the left. This road leads through a sandy hollow shaded by trees for about a quarter of a mile, where it crosses the bridge famous in goblin story; and just beyond swells the green knoll on which stands the whitewashed church.

As yet the panic of the steed had given his unskillful rider an apparent advantage in the chase, but just as he had got half way through the hollow, the girths of the saddle gave way, and he felt it slipping from under him. He seized it by the pommel, and endeavored to hold it firm, but in vain; and had just time to save himself by clasping old Gunpowder round the neck, when the saddle fell to the earth, and he heard it trampled under foot by his pursuer. For a moment the terror of Hans Van Ripper's wrath passed across his mind—for it was his Sunday saddle; but this was no time for petty fears; the goblin was hard on his haunches; and (unskillful rider that he was!) he had much ado to maintain his seat; sometimes slipping on one side, sometimes on another, and sometimes jolted on the high ridge of his horse's backbone, with a violence that he verily feared would cleave him asunder.

An opening in the trees now cheered him with the hopes that the church bridge was at hand. The wavering reflection of a silver star in the bosom of the brook told him that he was not mistaken. He saw the walls of the church dimly glaring under the trees beyond. He recollected the place where Brom Bones's ghostly competitor had disappeared. "If I can but reach that bridge," thought Ichabod, "I am safe." Just then he heard the black steed panting and blowing close behind him; he even fancied that he felt his hot breath. Another convulsive kick in the ribs, and old Gunpowder sprang upon the bridge; he thundered over the resounding planks; he gained the opposite side; and now Ichabod cast a look behind to see if his pursuer should vanish, according to rule, in a flash of fire and brimstone. Just then he saw the goblin rising in his stirrups, and in the very act of hurling his head at him. Ichabod endeavored to dodge the horrible missile, but too late. It encountered his cranium with a tremendous crash,—he was tumbled headlong into the dust, and Gunpowder, the black steed, and the goblin rider, passed by like a whirlwind.

The next morning the old horse was found without his saddle, and with the bridle under his feet, soberly cropping the grass at his master's gate. Ichabod did not make his appearance at breakfast; dinner-hour came, but no Ichabod. The boys assembled at the schoolhouse, and strolled idly about the banks of the brook; but no schoolmaster. Hans Van Ripper now began to feel some uneasiness about the fate of poor Ichabod, and his saddle. An inquiry was set on foot, and after diligent investigation they came upon his traces. In one part of the road leading to the church was found the saddle trampled in the dirt; the tracks of horses' hoofs deeply dented in the road, and evidently at furious speed, were traced to the bridge, beyond which, on the bank of a broad part of the brook, where the water ran deep and black, was found the hat of the unfortunate Ichabod, and close beside it a shattered pumpkin.

The Terrible Old Man

By H. P. Lovecraft

It was the design of Angelo Ricci and Joe Czanek and Manuel Silva to call on the Terrible Old Man. This old man dwells all alone in a very ancient house on Water Street near the sea, and is reputed to be both exceedingly rich and exceedingly feeble; which forms a situation very attractive to men of the profession of Messrs. Ricci, Czanek, and Silva, for that profession was nothing less dignified than robbery.

The inhabitants of Kingsport say and think many things about the Terrible Old Man which generally keep him safe from the attention of gentlemen like Mr. Ricci and his colleagues, despite the almost certain fact that he hides a fortune of indefinite magnitude somewhere about his musty and venerable abode. He is, in truth, a very strange person, believed to have been a captain of East India clipper ships in his day; so old that no one can remember when he was young, and so taciturn that few know his real name. Among the gnarled trees in the front yard of his aged and neglected place he maintains a strange collection of large stones, oddly grouped and painted so that they resemble the idols in some obscure Eastern temple. This collection frightens away most of the small boys who love to taunt the Terrible Old Man about his long white hair and beard, or to break the small-paned windows of his dwelling with wicked missiles; but there are other things which frighten the older and more curious folk who sometimes steal up to the house to peer in through the dusty panes. These folk say that on a table in a bare room on the ground floor are many peculiar bottles, in each a small piece of lead suspended pendulum-wise from a string. And they say that the Terrible Old Man talks to these bottles, addressing them by such names as Jack, Scar-Face, Long Tom, Spanish Joe, Peters, and Mate Ellis, and that whenever he speaks to a bottle the little lead pendulum within makes certain definite vibrations as if in answer.

Those who have watched the tall, lean, Terrible Old Man in these peculiar conversations, do not watch him again. But Angelo Ricci and Joe Czanek and Manuel Silva were not of Kingsport blood; they were of that new and heterogeneous alien stock which lies outside the charmed circle of New England life and traditions, and they saw in the Terrible Old Man merely a tottering, almost helpless gray-beard, who could not walk without the aid of his knotted cane, and whose thin, weak hands shook pitifully. They were really quite sorry in their way for the lonely, unpopular old fellow, whom everybody shunned, and at whom all the dogs barked singularly. But business is business, and to a robber whose soul is in his profession, there is a lure and a challenge about a very old and very feeble man who has no account at the bank, and who pays for his few necessities at the village store with Spanish gold and silver minted two centuries ago.

Messrs. Ricci, Czanek, and Silva selected the night of April 11th for their call. Mr. Ricci and Mr. Silva were to interview the poor old gentleman, while Mr. Czanek waited for them and their presumable metallic burden with a covered motor-car in Ship Street, by the gate in the tall rear wall of their host's grounds. Desire to avoid needless explanations in case of unexpected police intrusions prompted these plans for a quiet and unostentatious departure.

As prearranged, the three adventurers started out separately in order to prevent any evil-minded suspicions afterward. Messrs. Ricci and Silva met in Water Street by the old man's front gate, and although they did not like the way the moon shone down upon the painted stones through the budding branches of the gnarled trees, they had more important things to think about than mere idle superstition. They feared it might be unpleasant work making the Terrible Old Man loquacious concerning his hoarded gold and silver, for aged sea-captains are notably stubborn and perverse. Still, he was very old and very feeble, and there were two visitors. Messrs. Ricci and Silva were experienced in the art of making unwilling persons voluble, and the

The Terrible Old Man.

screams of a weak and exceptionally venerable man can be easily muffled. So they moved up to the one lighted window and heard the Terrible Old Man talking childishly to his bottles with pendulums. Then they donned masks and knocked politely at the weather-stained oaken door.

Waiting seemed very long to Mr. Czanek as he fidgeted restlessly in the covered motor-car by the Terrible Old Man's back gate in Ship Street. He was more than ordinarily tender-hearted, and he did not like the hideous screams he had heard in the ancient house just after the hour appointed for the deed. Had he not told his colleagues to be as gentle as possible with the pathetic old sea-captain? Very nervously he watched that narrow oaken gate in the high and ivy-clad stone wall. Frequently he consulted his watch, and wondered at the delay. Had the old man died before revealing where his treasure was hidden, and had a thorough search become necessary? Mr. Czanek did not like to wait so long in the dark in such a place. Then he sensed a soft tread or tapping on the walk inside the gate, heard a gentle fumbling at the rusty latch, and saw the narrow, heavy door swing inward. And in the pallid glow of the single dim street-lamp he strained his eyes to see what his colleagues had brought out of that sinister house which loomed so close behind. But when he looked, he did not see what he had expected; for his colleagues were not there at all, but only the Terrible Old Man leaning quietly on his knotted cane and smiling hideously. Mr. Czanek had never before noticed the color of that man's eyes; now he saw that they were yellow.

Little things make considerable excitement in little towns, which is the reason that Kingsport people talked all that spring and summer about the three unidentifiable bodies, horribly slashed as with many cutlasses, and horribly mangled as by the tread of many cruel boot-heels, which the tide washed in. And some people even spoke of things as trivial as the deserted motor-car found in Ship Street, or certain especially inhuman cries, probably of a stray animal or migratory bird, heard in the night by wakeful citizens. But in this idle village gossip the Terrible Old Man took no interest at all. He was by nature reserved, and when one is aged and feeble, one's reserve is doubly strong. Besides, so ancient a sea-captain must have witnessed scores of things much more stirring in the far-off days of his unremembered youth.

John Charrington's Wedding

By E. Nesbit

No one ever thought that May Forster would marry John Charrington; but he thought differently, and things which John Charrington intended had a queer way of coming to pass. He asked her to marry him before he went up to Oxford. She laughed and refused him. He asked her again next time he came home. Again she laughed, tossed her dainty blonde head and again refused. A third time he asked her; she said it was becoming a confirmed bad habit, and laughed at him more than ever.

John was not the only man who wanted to marry her: she was the belle of our village coterie, and we were all in love with her more or less; it was a sort of fashion, like heliotrope ties or Inverness capes. Therefore we were as much annoyed as surprised when John Charrington walked into our little local Club—we held it in a loft over the saddler's, I remember—and invited us all to his wedding.

"Your wedding?"

"You don't mean it?"

"Who's the happy pair? When's it to be?"

John Charrington filled his pipe and lighted it before he replied. Then he said:

"I'm sorry to deprive you fellows of your only joke—but Miss Forster and I are to be married in September."

"You don't mean it?"

"He's got the mitten again, and it's turned his head."

"No," I said, rising, "I see it's true. Lend me a pistol someone—or a first-class fare to the other end of Nowhere. Charrington has bewitched the only pretty girl in our twenty-mile radius. Was it mesmerism, or a love-potion, Jack?"

"Neither, sir, but a gift you'll never have—perseverance—and the best luck a man ever had in this world."

There was something in his voice that silenced me, and all chaff of the other fellows failed to draw him further.

The queer thing about it was that when we congratulated Miss Forster, she blushed and smiled and dimpled, for all the world as though she were in love with him, and had been in love with him all the time. Upon my word, I think she had. Women are strange creatures.

We were all asked to the wedding. In Brixham everyone who was anybody knew everybody else who was anyone. My sisters were, I truly believe, more interested in the trousseau than the bride herself, and I was to be best man. The coming marriage was much canvassed at afternoon tea-tables, and at our little Club over the saddler's, and the question was always asked, "Does she care for him?"

I used to ask that question myself in the early days of their engagement, but after a certain evening in August I never asked it again. I was coming home from the Club through the churchyard. Our church is on a thyme-grown hill, and the turf about it is so thick and soft that one's footsteps are noiseless.

I made no sound as I vaulted the low lichened wall, and threaded my way between the tombstones. It was at the same instant that I heard John Charrington's voice, and saw her. May was sitting on a low flat gravestone, her face turned towards the full splendor of the western sun. Its expression ended, at once and for ever, any question of love for him; it was transfigured to a beauty I should not have believed possible, even to that beautiful little face.

John lay at her feet, and it was his voice that broke the stillness of the golden August evening.

"My dear, my dear, I believe I should come back from the dead if you wanted me!"

I coughed at once to indicate my presence, and passed on into the shadow fully enlightened.

"I should come back from the dead."

The wedding was to be early in September. Two days before I had to run up to town on business. The train was late, of course, for we are on the South-Eastern, and as I stood grumbling with my watch in my hand, whom should I see but John Charrington and May Forster. They were walking up and down the unfrequented end of the platform, arm in arm, looking into each other's eyes, careless of the sympathetic interest of the porters.

Of course I knew better than to hesitate a moment before burying myself in the booking-office, and it was not till the train drew up at the platform, that I obtrusively passed the pair with my Gladstone, and took the corner in a first-class smoking-carriage. I did this with as good an air of not seeing them as I could assume. I pride myself on my discretion, but if John were traveling alone I wanted his company. I had it.

"Hullo, old man," came his cheery voice as he swung his bag into my carriage; "here's luck; I was expecting a dull journey!"

"Where are you off to?" I asked, discretion still bidding me turn my eyes away, though I saw, without looking, that hers were red-rimmed.

"To old Branbridge's," he answered, shutting the door and leaning out for a last word with his sweetheart.

"Oh, I wish you wouldn't go, John," she was saying in a low, earnest voice. "I feel certain something will happen."

"Do you think I should let anything happen to keep me, and the day after tomorrow our wedding day?"

"Don't go," she answered, with a pleading intensity which would have sent my Gladstone onto the platform and me after it. But she wasn't speaking to me. John Charrington was made differently: he rarely changed his opinions, never his resolutions.

He only stroked the little ungloved hands that lay on the carriage door.

"I must, May. The old boy's been awfully good to me, and now he's dying I must go and see him, but I shall come home in time for—" the rest of the parting was lost in a whisper and in the rattling lurch of the starting train.

"You're sure to come?" she spoke as the train moved.

"Nothing shall keep me," he answered; and we steamed out. After he had seen the last of the little figure on the platform he leaned back in his corner and kept silence for a minute.

When he spoke it was to explain to me that his godfather, whose heir he was, lay dying at Peasmarsh Place, some fifty miles away, and had sent for John, and John had felt bound to go.

"I shall be surely back tomorrow," he said, "or, if not, the day after, in heaps of time. Thank heaven, one hasn't to get up in the middle of the night to get married nowadays!"

"And suppose Mr. Branbridge dies?"

"Alive or dead I mean to be married on Thursday!" John answered, lighting a cigar and unfolding *The Times.*

At Peasmarsh station we said "goodbye," and he got out, and I saw him ride off; I went on to London, where I stayed the night.

When I got home the next afternoon, a very wet one, by the way, my sister greeted me with:

"Where's Mr. Charrington?"

"Goodness knows," I answered testily. Every man, since Cain, has resented that kind of question.

"I thought you might have heard from him," she went on, "as you're to give him away tomorrow."

"Isn't he back?" I asked, for I had confidently expected to find him at home.

"No, Geoffrey," my sister Fanny always had a way of jumping to conclusions, especially such conclusions as were least favorable to her fellow-creatures—"he has not returned, and, what is more, you may depend upon it he won't. You mark my words, there'll be no wedding tomorrow."

My sister Fanny has a power of annoying me which no other human being possesses.

"You mark my words," I retorted with asperity, "you had better give up making such a thundering idiot of yourself. There'll be more wedding tomorrow than ever you'll take the first part in." A prophecy which, by the way, came true.

But though I could snarl confidently to my sister, I did not feel so comfortable when late that night, I, standing on the doorstep of John's house, heard that he had not returned. I went home gloomily through the rain. Next morning brought a brilliant blue sky, gold sun, and all such softness of air and beauty of cloud as go to make up a perfect day. I woke with a vague feeling of having gone to bed anxious, and of being rather averse to facing that anxiety in the light of full wakefulness.

But with my shaving-water came a note from John which relieved my mind and sent me up to the Forsters with a light heart.

May was in the garden. I saw her blue gown through the hollyhocks as the lodge gates swung to behind me. So I did not go up to the house, but turned aside down the turfed path.

"He's written to you too," she said, without preliminary greeting, when I reached her side.

"Yes, I'm to meet him at the station at three, and come straight on to the church."

Her face looked pale, but there was a brightness in her eyes, and a tender quiver about the mouth that spoke of renewed happiness.

"Mr. Branbridge begged him so to stay another night that he had not the heart to refuse," she went on. "He is so kind, but I wish he hadn't stayed."

I was at the station at half past two. I felt rather annoyed with John. It seemed a sort of slight to the beautiful girl who loved him, that he should come as it were out of breath, and with the dust of travel upon him, to take her hand, which some of us would have given the best years of our lives to take.

But when the three o'clock train glided in, and glided out again having brought no passengers to our little station, I was more than annoyed. There was no other train for thirty-five minutes; I calculated that, with much hurry, we might just get to the church in time for the ceremony; but, oh, what a fool to miss that first train! What other man could have done it?

That thirty-five minutes seemed a year, as I wandered round the station reading the advertisements and the timetables, and the company's bylaws, and getting more and more angry with John Charrington. This confidence in his own power of getting everything he wanted the minute he wanted it was leading him too far. I hate waiting. Everyone does, but I believe I hate it more than anyone else. The three thirty-five was late, of course.

"Drive to the church!" I said, as someone shut the door. "Mr. Charrington hasn't come by this train."

I ground my pipe between my teeth and stamped with impatience as I watched the signals. Click. The signal went down. Five minutes later I flung myself into the carriage that I had brought for John.

Anxiety now replaced anger. What had become of the man? Could he have been taken suddenly ill? I had never known him have a day's illness in his life. And even so he might have telegraphed. Some awful accident must have happened to him. The thought that he had played her false never—no, not for a moment—entered my head. Yes, something terrible had happened to him, and on me lay the task of telling his bride. I almost wished the carriage would upset and break my head so that someone else might tell her, not I, who—but that's nothing to do with this story.

It was five minutes to four as we drew up at the churchyard gate. A double row of eager onlookers lined the path from lych-gate to porch. I sprang from the carriage and passed up between them. Our gardener had a good front place near the door. I stopped.

"Are they waiting still, Byles?" I asked, simply to gain time, for of course I knew they were by the waiting crowd's attentive attitude.

"Waiting, sir? No, no, sir; why, it must be over by now."

"Over! Then Mr. Charrington's come?"

"To the minute, sir; must have missed you somehow, and I say, sir," lowering his voice, "I never see Mr. John the least bit so afore, but my opinion is he's been drinking pretty free. His clothes was all dusty and his face like a sheet. I tell you I didn't like the looks of him at all, and the folks inside are saying all sorts of things. You'll see, something's gone very wrong with Mr. John, and he's tried liquor. He looked like a ghost, and in he went with his eyes straight before him, with never a look or a word for none of us: him that was always such a gentleman!"

I had never heard Byles make so long a speech. The crowd in the churchyard were talking in whispers and getting ready rice and slippers to throw at the bride and bridegroom. The ringers were ready with their hands on the ropes to ring out the merry peal as the bride and bridegroom should come out.

A murmur from the church announced them; out they came. Byles was right. John Charrington did not look himself. There was dust on his coat, his hair was disarranged. He seemed to have been in some row, for there was a black mark above his eyebrow. He was deathly pale. But his pallor was not greater than that of the bride, who might have been carved in ivory—dress, veil, orange blossoms, face and all.

As they passed out the ringers stooped—there were six of them—and then, on the ears expecting the gay wedding peal, came the slow tolling of the passing bell.

A thrill of horror at so foolish a jest from the ringers passed through us all. But the ringers themselves dropped the ropes and fled like rabbits out into the sunlight. The bride shuddered, and gray shadows came about her mouth, but the bridegroom led her on down the path where the people stood with the handfuls of rice; but the handfuls were never thrown, and the wedding bells never rang. In vain the ringers were urged to remedy their mistake: they protested with many whispered expletives that they would see themselves further first.

In a hush like the hush in the chamber of death the bridal pair passed into their carriage and its door slammed behind them.

Then the tongues were loosed. A babel of anger, wonder, conjecture from the guests and the spectators.

"If I'd seen his condition, sir," said old Forster to me as we drove off, "I would have stretched him on the floor of the church, sir, by heaven I would, before I'd have let him marry my daughter!"

Then he put his head out of the window.

"Drive like hell," he cried to the coachman; "don't spare the horses."

He was obeyed. We passed the bride's carriage. I forbore to look at it, and old Forster turned his head away and swore. We reached home before it.

We stood in the doorway, in the blazing afternoon sun, and in about half a minute we heard wheels crunching the gravel. When the carriage stopped in front of the steps old Forster and I ran down.

"Great heaven, the carriage is empty! And yet—"

I had the door open in a minute, and this is what I saw . . .

No sign of John Charrington; and of May, his wife, only a huddled heap of white satin lying half on the floor of the carriage and half on the seat.

"I drove straight here, sir," said the coachman, as the bride's father lifted her out; "and I'll swear no one got out of the carriage."

We carried her into the house in her bridal dress and drew back her veil. I saw her face. Shall I ever forget it? White, white and drawn with agony and horror, bearing such a look of terror as I have never seen since except in dreams. And her hair, her radiant blonde hair, I tell you it was white like snow.

As we stood, her father and I, half mad with the horror and mystery of it, a boy came up the avenue—a telegraph boy. They brought the orange envelope to me. I tore it open.

Mr. Charrington was thrown from the dogcart on his way to the station at half past one. Killed on the spot!

And he was married to May Forster in our parish church at *half past three,* in presence of half the parish.

"I shall be married, dead, or alive!"

What had passed in that carriage on the homeward drive? No one knows—no one will ever know. Oh, May! oh, my dear!

Before a week was over they laid her beside her husband in our little churchyard on the thyme-covered hill—the churchyard where they had kept their love-trysts.

Thus was accomplished John Charrington's wedding.

The Furnished Room

By O. Henry

Restless, shifting, fugacious as time itself is a certain vast bulk of the population of the red brick district of the lower West Side. Homeless, they have a hundred homes. They flit from furnished room to furnished room, transients forever—transients in abode, transients in heart and mind. They sing "Home, Sweet Home" in ragtime; they carry their *lares et penates* in a bandbox; their vine is entwined about a picture hat; a rubber plant is their fig tree.

Hence the houses of this district, having had a thousand dwellers, should have a thousand tales to tell, mostly dull ones, no doubt; but it would be strange if there could not be found a ghost or two in the wake of all these vagrant guests.

One evening after dark a young man prowled among these crumbling red mansions, ringing their bells. At the twelfth he rested his lean hand-baggage upon the step and wiped the dust from his hatband and forehead. The bell sounded faint and far away in some remote, hollow depths.

To the door of this, the twelfth house whose bell he had rung, came a housekeeper who made him think of an unwholesome, surfeited worm that had eaten its nut to a hollow shell and now sought to fill the vacancy with edible lodgers.

He asked if there was a room to let.

"Come in," said the housekeeper. Her voice came from her throat; her throat seemed lined with fur. "I have the third-floor-back, vacant since a week back. Should you wish to look at it?"

The young man followed her up the stairs. A faint light from no particular source mitigated the shadows of the halls. They trod noiselessly upon a stair carpet that its own loom would have forsworn. It seemed to have become vegetable; to have degenerated in that rank, sunless air to lush lichen or spreading moss that grew in patches to the staircase and was viscid under the foot like organic matter. At each turn of the stairs were vacant niches in the wall. Perhaps plants had once been set within them. If so they had died in that foul and tainted air. It may be that statues of the saints had stood there, but it was not difficult to conceive that imps and devils had dragged them forth in the darkness and down to the unholy depths of some furnished pit below.

"This is the room," said the housekeeper, from her furry throat. "It's a nice room. It ain't often vacant. I had some most elegant people in it last summer—no trouble at all, and paid in advance to the minute. The water's at the end of the hall. Sprowls and Mooney kept it three months. They done a vaudeville sketch. Miss B'retta Sprowls—you may have heard of her—oh, that was just the stage names—right there over the dresser is where the marriage certificate hung, framed. The gas is here, and you see there is plenty of closet room. It's a room everybody likes. It never stays idle long."

"Do you have many theatrical people rooming here?" asked the young man.

"They comes and goes. A good proportion of my lodgers is connected with the theaters. Yes, sir, this is the theatrical district. Actor people never stays long anywhere. I get my share. Yes, they comes and they goes."

He engaged the room, paying for a week in advance. He was tired, he said, and would take possession at once. He counted out the money. The room had been made ready, she said, even to towels and water. As the housekeeper moved away he put, for the thousandth time, the question that he carried at the end of his tongue.

"A young girl—Miss Vashner—Miss Eloise Vashner—do you remember such a one among your lodgers? She would be singing on the stage, most likely. A fair girl, of medium height and slender, with reddish, gold hair and a dark mole near her left eyebrow."

"No, I don't remember the name. Them stage people has names they change as often as their rooms. They comes and they goes. No, I don't call that one to mind."

No. Always no. Five months of ceaseless interrogation and the inevitable negative. So much time spent by day in questioning managers, agents, schools, and choruses; by night among the audiences of theaters from all-star casts down to music halls so low that he dreaded to find what he most hoped for. He who had loved her best had tried to find her. He was sure that since her disappearance from home this great, water-girt city held her somewhere, but it was like a monstrous quicksand, shifting its particles constantly, with no foundation, its upper granules of today buried tomorrow in ooze and slime.

The furnished room received its latest guest with a first glow of pseudo-hospitality, a hectic, haggard, perfunctory welcome like the specious smile of a demirep. The sophistical comfort came in reflected gleams from the decayed furniture, the ragged brocade upholstery of a couch and two chairs, a foot-wide cheap pier glass between the two windows, from one or two gilt picture frames and a brass bedstead in a corner.

The guest reclined, inert, upon a chair, while the room, confused in speech as though it were an apartment in Babel, tried to discourse to him of its diverse tenantry.

A polychromatic rug like some brilliant-flowered rectangular, tropical islet lay surrounded by a billowy sea of soiled matting. Upon the gay-papered wall were those pictures that pursue the homeless one from house to house—The Huguenot Lovers, The First Quarrel, The Wedding Breakfast, Psyche at the Fountain. The mantel's chastely severe outline was ingloriously veiled behind some pert drapery drawn rakishly askew like the sashes of the Amazonian ballet. Upon it was some desolate flotsam cast aside by the room's marooned when a lucky sail had borne them to a fresh port—a trifling vase or two, pictures of actresses, a medicine bottle, some stray cards out of a deck.

One by one, as the characters of a cryptograph become explicit, the little signs left by the furnished room's procession of guests developed a significance. The threadbare space in the rug in front of the dresser told that lovely woman had marched in the throng. Tiny finger prints on the wall spoke of little prisoners trying to feel their way to sun and air. A splattered stain, raying like the shadow of a bursting bomb, witnessed where a hurled glass or bottle had splintered with its contents against the wall. Across the pier glass had been scrawled with a diamond in staggering letters the name

"Marie." It seemed that the succession of dwellers in the furnished room had turned in fury—perhaps tempted beyond forbearance by its garish coldness—and wreaked upon it their passions. The furniture was chipped and bruised; the couch, distorted by bursting springs, seemed a horrible monster that had been slain during the stress of some grotesque convulsion. Some more potent upheaval had cloven a great slice from the marble mantel. Each plank in the floor owned its particular cant and shriek as from a separate and individual agony. It seemed incredible that all this malice and injury had been wrought upon the room by those who had called it for a time their home; and yet it may have been the cheated home instinct surviving blindly, the resentful rage at false household gods that had kindled their wrath. A hut that is our own we can sweep and adorn and cherish.

The young tenant in the chair allowed these thoughts to file, soft-shod, through his mind, while there drifted into the room furnished sounds and furnished scents. He heard in one room a tittering and incontinent, slack laughter; in others the monologue of a scold, the rattling of dice, a lullaby, and one crying dully; above him a banjo tinkled with spirit. Doors banged somewhere; the elevated trains roared intermittently; a cat yowled miserably upon a back fence. And he breathed the breath of the house—a dank savor rather than a smell—a cold, musty effluvium as from underground vaults mingled with the reeking exhalations of linoleum and mildewed and rotten woodwork.

Then, suddenly, as he rested there, the room was filled with the strong, sweet odor of mignonette. It came as upon a single buffet of wind with such sureness and fragrance and emphasis that it almost seemed a living visitant. And the man cried aloud: "What, dear?" as if he had been called, and sprang up and faced about. The rich odor clung to him and wrapped him around. He reached out his arms for it, all his senses for the time confused and commingled. How could one be peremptorily called by an odor? Surely it must have been a sound. But, was it not the sound that had touched, that had caressed him?

"She has been in this room," he cried, and he sprang to wrest from it a token, for he knew he would recognize the smallest thing that had belonged to her or that she had touched. This enveloping scent of mignonette, the odor that she had loved and made her own—whence came it?

Oh, God! whence that odor?

The room had been but carelessly set in order. Scattered upon the flimsy dresser scarf were half a dozen hairpins—those discreet, indistinguishable friends of womankind, feminine of gender, infinite of mood and uncommunicative of tense. These he ignored, conscious of their triumphant lack of identity. Ransacking the drawers of the dresser he came upon a discarded, tiny, ragged handkerchief. He pressed it to his face. It was racy and insolent with heliotrope; he hurled it to the floor. In another drawer he found odd buttons, a theater program, a pawnbroker's card, two lost marshmallows, a book on the divination of dreams. In the last was a woman's black satin hair bow, which halted him, poised between ice and fire. But the black satin hair-bow also is femininity's demure, impersonal, common ornament, and tells no tales.

And then he traversed the room like a hound on the scent, skimming the walls, considering the corners of the bulging matting on his hands and knees, rummaging mantel and tables, the curtains and hangings, the drunken cabinet in the corner, for a visible sign, unable to perceive that she was there beside, around, against, within, above him, clinging to him, wooing him, calling him so poignantly through the finer senses that even his grosser ones became cognizant of the call. Once again he answered loudly: "Yes, dear!" and turned, wild-eyed, to gaze on vacancy, for he could not yet discern form and color and love and outstretched arms in the odor of mignonette. Oh, God! whence that odor, and since when had odors had a voice to call? Thus he groped.

He burrowed in crevices and corners, and found corks and cigarettes. These he passed in passive contempt. But once he found in a fold of the matting a half-smoked cigar, and this he ground beneath his heel with a green and trenchant oath. He sifted the room from end to end. He found dreary and ignoble small records of many a peripatetic tenant; but of her whom he sought, and who may have lodged there, and whose spirit seemed to hover there, he found no trace.

And then he thought of the housekeeper.

He ran from the haunted room downstairs and to a door that showed a crack of light. She came out to his knock. He smothered his excitement as best he could.

"Will you tell me, madam," he besought her, "who occupied the room I have before I came?"

"Yes, sir. I can tell you again. 'Twas Sprowls and Mooney, as I said. Miss B'retta Sprowls it was in the theaters, but Missis Mooney she was. My house is well known for respectability. The marriage certificate hung, framed, on a nail over—"

"What kind of a lady was Miss Sprowls—in looks, I mean?"

"Why, black-haired, sir, short, and stout, with a comical face. They left a week ago Tuesday."

"And before they occupied it?"

"Why, there was a single gentleman connected with the draying business. He left owing me a week. Before him was Missis Crowder and her two children, that stayed four months; and back of them was old Mr. Doyle, whose sons paid for him. He kept the room six months. That goes back a year, sir, and further I do not remember."

He thanked her and crept back to his room. The room was dead. The essence that had vivified it was gone. The perfume of mignonette had departed. In its place was the old, stale odor of moldy house furniture, of atmosphere in storage.

The ebbing of his hope drained his faith. He sat staring at the yellow, singing gaslight. Soon he walked to the bed and began to tear the sheets into strips. With the blade of his knife he drove them tightly into every crevice around windows and door. When all was snug and taut he turned off the light, turned the gas full on again and laid himself gratefully upon the bed.

—

It was Mrs. McCool's night to go with the can for beer. So she fetched it and sat with Mrs. Purdy in one of those subterranean retreats where housekeepers foregather and the worm dieth seldom.

"I rented out my third floor, back, this evening," said Mrs. Purdy, across a fine circle of foam. "A young man took it. He went up to bed two hours ago."

"Now, did ye, Mrs. Purdy, ma'am?" said Mrs. McCool, with intense admiration. "You do be a wonder for rentin' rooms of that kind. And did ye tell him, then?" she concluded in a husky whisper, laden with mystery.

"Rooms," said Mrs. Purdy, in her furriest tones, "are furnished for to rent. I did not tell him, Mrs. McCool."

"'Tis right ye are, ma'am; 'tis by renting rooms we kape alive. Ye have the rale sense for business, ma'am. There be many people will rayjict the rentin' of a room if they be told a suicide has been after dyin' in the bed of it."

"As you say, we has our living to be making," remarked Mrs. Purdy.

"Yis, ma'am; 'tis true. 'Tis just one wake ago this day I helped ye lay out the third floor, back. A pretty slip of a colleen she was to be killin' herself wid the gas—a swate little face she had, Mrs. Purdy, ma'am."

"She'd a-been called handsome, as you say," said Mrs. Purdy, assenting but critical, "but for that mole she had a-growin' by her left eyebrow. Do fill up your glass again, Mrs. McCool."

The Man Upstairs

By Ray Bradbury

He remembered how carefully and expertly Grandmother would fondle the cold cut guts of the chicken and withdraw the marvels therein; the wet shining loops of meat-smelling intestine, the muscled lump of heart, the gizzard with the collection of seeds in it. How neatly and nicely Grandma would slit the chicken and push her fat little hand in to deprive it of its medals. These would be segregated, some in pans of water, others in paper to be thrown to the dog later, perhaps. And then the ritual of taxidermy, stuffing the bird with watered, seasoned bread, and performing surgery with a swift, bright needle, stitch after pulled-tight stitch.

This was one of the prime thrills of Douglas's eleven-year-old life span.

Altogether, he counted twenty knives in the various squealing drawers of the magic kitchen table from which Grandma, a kindly, gentle-faced, white-haired old witch, drew paraphernalia for her miracles.

Douglas was to be quiet. He could stand across the table from Grandma, his freckled nose tucked over the edge, watching, but any loose boy-talk might interfere with the spell. It was a wonder when Grandma brandished silver shakers over the bird, supposedly sprinkling showers of mummy-dust and pulverized Indian bones, muttering mystical verses under her toothless breath.

"Grammy," said Douglas at last, breaking the silence. "Am I like that inside?" He pointed at the chicken.

"Yes," said Grandma. "A little more orderly and presentable, but just about the same. . . ."

"And more *of* it!" added Douglas, proud of his guts.

"Yes," said Grandma. "More of it."

"Grandpa has lots more'n me. His sticks out in front so he can rest his elbows on it."

Grandma laughed and shook her head.

Douglas said, "And Lucie Williams, down the street, she . . ."

"Hush, child!" cried Grandma.

"But she's got . . ."

"Never you mind what she's got! That's different."

"But why is *she* different?"

"A darning-needle dragon-fly is coming by some day and sew up your mouth," said Grandma firmly.

Douglas waited, then asked, "How do you know I've got insides like that, Grandma?"

"Oh, go 'way, now!"

The front doorbell rang.

Through the front-door glass as he ran down the hall, Douglas saw a straw hat. The bell jangled again and again. Douglas opened the door.

"Good morning, child, is the landlady at home?"

Cold gray eyes in a long, smooth, walnut-colored face gazed upon Douglas. The man was tall, thin, and carried a suitcase, a briefcase, an umbrella under one bent arm, gloves rich and thick and gray on his thin fingers, and wore a horribly new straw hat.

Douglas backed up. "She's busy."

"I wish to rent her upstairs room, as advertised."

"We've got ten boarders, and it's already rented; go away!"

"Douglas!" Grandma was behind him suddenly. "How do you do?" she said to the stranger. "Never mind this child."

Unsmiling, the man stepped stiffly in. Douglas watched them ascend out of sight up the stairs, heard Grandma detailing the conveniences of the upstairs room. Soon she hurried down to pile linens from the linen closet on Douglas and send him scooting up with them.

Douglas paused at the room's threshold. The room was changed oddly, simply because the stranger had been in it a moment. The straw hat lay brittle and terrible upon the bed, the umbrella leaned stiff against one wall like a dead bat with dark wings folded.

Douglas blinked at the umbrella.

The stranger stood in the center of the changed room, tall, tall.

"Here!" Douglas littered the bed with supplies. "We eat at noon sharp, and if you're late coming down the soup'll get cold. Grandma fixes it so it will, every time!"

The tall strange man counted out ten new copper pennies and tinkled them in Douglas's blouse pocket. "We shall be friends," he said, grimly.

It was funny, the man having nothing but pennies. Lots of them. No silver at all, no dimes, no quarters. Just new copper pennies.

Douglas thanked him glumly. "I'll drop these in my dime bank when I get them changed into a dime. I got six dollars and fifty cents in dimes all ready for my camp trip in August."

"I must wash now," said the tall strange man.

Once, at midnight, Douglas had wakened to hear a storm rumbling outside—the cold hard wind shaking the house, the rain driving against the window. And then a lightning bolt had landed outside the window with a silent, terrific concussion. He remembered that fear of looking about at his room, seeing it strange and awful in the instantaneous light.

So it was, now, in this room. He stood looking up at the stranger. This room was no longer the same, but changed indefinably because this man, quick as a lightning bolt, had shed his light about it. Douglas backed up slowly as the stranger advanced.

The door closed in his face.

The wooden fork went up with mashed potatoes, came down empty. Mr. Koberman, for that was his name, had brought the wooden fork and wooden knife and spoon with him when Grandma called lunch.

"Mrs. Spaulding," he said, quietly, "my own cutlery; please use it. I will have lunch today, but from tomorrow on, only breakfast and supper."

Grandma bustled in and out, bearing steaming tureens of soup and beans and mashed potatoes to impress her new border, while Douglas sat rattling his silverware on his plate, because he had discovered it irritated Mr. Koberman.

"I know a trick," said Douglas. "Watch." He picked a fork-tine with his fingernail. He pointed at various sectors of the table, like a magician. Wherever he pointed, the sound of the vibrating fork-tine emerged, like a metal elfin voice. Simply done, of course. He pressed the fork handle on the tabletop, secretly. The vibration came from the wood like a sounding board. It looked quite magical. "There, there, and *there!*" exclaimed Douglas, happily plucking the fork again. He pointed at Mr. Koberman's soup and the noise came from it.

Mr. Koberman's walnut-colored face became hard and firm and awful. He pushed the soup bowl away violently, his lips twisting. He fell back in his chair.

Grandma appeared. "Why, what's wrong, Mr. Koberman?"

"I cannot eat this soup."

"Why?"

"Because I am full and can eat no more. Thank you."

Mr. Koberman left the room, glaring.

"What did you do, just then?" asked Grandma at Douglas, sharply.

"Nothing. Grandma, why does he eat with *wooden* spoons?"

"Yours not to question! When do you go back to school, anyway?"

"Seven weeks."

"Oh, my land!" said Grandma.

Mr. Koberman worked nights. Each morning at eight he arrived mysteriously home, devoured a very small breakfast, and then slept soundlessly in his room all through the dreaming hot daytime, until the huge supper with all the other boarders at night.

Mr. Koberman's sleeping habits made it necessary for Douglas to be quiet. This was unbearable. So, whenever Grandma visited down the street, Douglas stomped up and down stairs beating a drum, bouncing golf balls, or just screaming for three minutes outside Mr. Koberman's door, or flushing the toilet seven times in succession.

Mr. Koberman never moved. His room was silent, dark. He did not complain. There was no sound. He slept on and on. It was very strange.

Douglas felt a pure white flame of hatred burn inside himself with a steady, unflickering beauty. Now that room was Koberman Land. Once it had been flowery bright when Miss Sadlowe lived there. Now it was stark, bare, cold, clean, everything in its place, alien and brittle.

Douglas climbed upstairs on the fourth morning.

Halfway to the second floor was a large sun-filled window, framed by six-inch panes of orange, purple, blue, red and burgundy glass. In the enchanted early mornings when the sun fell through to strike the landing and slide down the stair banister, Douglas stood entranced at this window peering at the world through the multicolored panes.

Now a blue world, a blue sky, blue people, blue streetcars, and blue trotting dogs.

He shifted panes. Now—an amber world! Two lemonish women glided by, resembling the daughters of Fu Manchu! Douglas giggled. This pane made even the sunlight more purely golden.

It was eight A.M. Mr. Koberman strolled by below, on the sidewalk, returning from his night's work, his umbrella looped over his elbow, straw hat glued to his head with patent oil.

Douglas shifted panes again. Mr. Koberman was a red man walking through a red world with red trees and red flowers and—something else.

Something about—Mr. Koberman.

Douglas squinted.

The red glass *did* things to Mr. Koberman. His face, his suit, his hands. The clothes seemed to melt away. Douglas almost believed, for one terrible instant, that he could see *inside* Mr. Koberman. And what he saw made him lean wildly against the small red pane, blinking.

Mr. Koberman glanced up just then, saw Douglas, and raised his umbrella angrily, as if to strike. He ran swiftly across the red lawn to the front door.

"Young man!" he cried, running up the stairs. "What were you doing?"

"Just looking," said Douglas, numbly.

"That's all, is it?" cried Mr. Koberman.

"Yes, sir. I look through all the glasses. All kinds of worlds. Blue ones, red ones, yellow ones. All different."

"All kinds of worlds, is it!" Mr. Koberman glanced at the little panes of glass, his face pale. He got hold of himself. He wiped his face with a handkerchief and pretended to laugh. "Yes. All kinds of worlds. All different." He walked to the door of his room. "Go right ahead; play," he said.

The door closed. The hall was empty. Mr. Koberman had gone in.

Douglas shrugged and found a new pane.

"Oh, everything's violet!"

Half an hour later, while playing in his sandbox behind the house, Douglas heard the crash and the shattering tinkle. He leaped up.

A moment later, Grandma appeared on the back porch, the old razor strop trembling in her hand.

"Douglas! I told you time and again never fling your basketball against the house! Oh, I could just cry!"

"I been sitting right here," he protested.

"Come see what you've done, you nasty boy!"

The great colored windowpanes lay shattered in a rainbow chaos on the upstairs landing. His basketball lay in the ruins.

Before he could even begin telling his innocence, Douglas was struck a dozen stinging blows upon his rump. Wherever he landed, screaming, the razor strop struck again.

Later, hiding his mind in the sandpile like an ostrich, Douglas nursed his dreadful pains. He knew who'd thrown that basketball. A man with a straw hat and a stiff umbrella and a cold, gray room. Yeah, yeah, yeah. He dribbled tears. Just wait. Just *wait.*

He heard Grandma sweeping up the broken glass. She brought it out and threw it in the trash bin. Blue, pink, yellow meteors of glass dropped brightly down.

When she was gone, Douglas dragged himself, whimpering, over to save out three pieces of the incredible glass. Mr. Koberman disliked the colored windows. These—he clinked them in his fingers—would be worth saving.

Grandfather arrived from his newspaper office each night, shortly ahead of the other boarders, at five o'clock. When a slow, heavy tread filled the hall, and a thick, mahogany cane thumped in the cane-rack, Douglas ran to embrace the large stomach and sit on Grandpa's knee while he read the evening paper.

"Hi, Grampa!"

"Hello, down there!"

"Grandma cut chickens again today. It's fun watching," said Douglas.

Grandpa kept reading. "That's twice this week, chickens. She's the chickenist woman. You like to watch her cut 'em, eh? Cold-blooded little pepper! Ha!"

"I'm just curious."

"You are," rumbled Grandpa, scowling. "Remember that day when that young lady was killed at the rail station? You just walked over and looked at her, blood and all." He laughed. "Queer duck. Stay that way. Fear nothing, ever in your life. I guess you get it from your father, him being a military man and all, and you so close to him before you came here to live last year." Grandpa returned to his paper.

A long pause. "Gramps?"

"Yes?"

"What if a man didn't have a heart or lungs or stomach but still walked around, alive?"

"That," rumbled Gramps, "would be a miracle."

"I don't mean a—miracle. I mean, what if he was all *different* inside? Not like me."

"Well, he wouldn't be quite human then, would he, boy?"

"Guess not, Gramps. Gramps, you got a heart and lungs?"

Gramps chuckled. "Well, tell the truth, I don't *know*. Never seen them. Never had an X-ray, never been to a doctor. Might as well be potato-solid for all I know."

"Have *I* got a stomach?"

"You certainly have!" cried Grandma from the parlor entry. "'Cause I feed it! And you've lungs, you scream loud enough to wake the crumblees. And you've dirty hands, go wash them! Dinner's ready. Grandpa, come on. Douglas, git!"

In the rush of boarders streaming downstairs, Grandpa, if he intended questioning Douglas further about the weird conversation, lost his opportunity. If dinner delayed an instant more, Grandma and the potatoes would develop simultaneous lumps.

The boarders, laughing and talking at the table—Mr. Koberman silent and sullen among them—were silenced when Grandfather cleared his throat. He talked politics a few minutes and then shifted over into the intriguing topic of the recent peculiar deaths in the town.

"It's enough to make an old newspaper editor prick up his ears," he said, eyeing them all. "That young Miss Larson, lived across the ravine, now. Found her dead three days ago for no reason, just funny kinds of tattoos all over her, and a facial expression that would make Dante cringe. And that other young lady, what was her name? Whitely? She disappeared and *never did* come back."

"Them things happen alla time," said Mr. Britz, the garage mechanic, chewing. "Ever peek inna Missing People Bureau file? It's *that* long." He illustrated. "Can't tell *what* happens to most of 'em."

"Anyone want more dressing?" Grandma ladled liberal portions from the chicken's interior. Douglas watched, thinking about how that chicken had had two kinds of guts—God-made and Man-made.

Well, how about *three* kinds of guts?

Eh?

Why not?

Conversation continued about the mysterious death of so-and-so, and, oh, yes, remember a week ago, Marion Barsumian died of heart failure, but maybe that didn't connect up? or did it? you're crazy! forget it, why talk about it at the dinner table? So.

"Never can tell," said Mr. Britz. "Maybe we got a vampire in town."

Mr. Koberman stopped eating.

"In the year 1927?" said Grandma. "A vampire? Oh go on, now."

"Sure," said Mr. Britz. "Kill 'em with silver bullets. Anything silver for that matter. Vampires *hate* silver. I read it in a book somewhere, once. Sure, I did."

Douglas looked at Mr. Koberman who ate with wooden knives and forks and carried only new copper pennies in his pocket.

"It's poor judgment," said Grandpa, "to call anything by a name. We don't know what a hobgoblin or a vampire or a troll is. Could be lots of things.

You can't heave them into categories with labels and say they'll act one way or another. That'd be silly. They're people. People who do things. Yes, that's the way to put it: people who *do* things."

"Excuse me," said Mr. Koberman, who got up and went out for his evening walk to work.

The stars, the moon, the wind, the clock ticking, and the chiming of the hours into dawn, the sun rising, and here it was another morning, another day, and Mr. Koberman coming along the sidewalk from his night's work. Douglas stood off like a small mechanism whirring and watching with carefully microscopic eyes.

At noon, Grandma went to the store to buy groceries.

As was his custom every day when Grandma was gone, Douglas yelled outside Mr. Koberman's door for a full three minutes. As usual, there was no response. The silence was horrible.

He ran downstairs, got the pass-key, a silver fork, and the three pieces of colored glass he had saved from the shattered window. He fitted the key to the lock and swung the door slowly open.

The room was in half light, the shades drawn. Mr. Koberman lay atop his bedcovers, in slumber clothes, breathing gently, up and down. He didn't move. His face was motionless.

"Hello, Mr. Koberman!"

The colorless walls echoed the man's regular breathing.

"Mr. Koberman, hello!"

Bouncing a golf ball, Douglas advanced. He yelled. Still no answer. "Mr. Koberman!"

Bending over Mr. Koberman, Douglas picked the tines of the silver fork in the sleeping man's face.

Mr. Koberman winced. He twisted. He groaned bitterly.

Response. Good. Swell.

Douglas drew a piece of blue glass from his pocket. Looking through the blue glass fragment he found himself in a blue room, in a blue world different from the world he knew. As different as was the red world. Blue furniture,

Mr. Koberman winced.

blue bed, blue ceiling and walls, blue wooden eating utensils atop the blue bureau, and the sullen dark blue of Mr. Koberman's face and arms and his blue chest rising, falling. Also . . .

Mr. Koberman's eyes were wide, staring at him with a hungry darkness.

Douglas fell back, pulled the blue glass from his eyes.

Mr. Koberman's eyes were shut.

Blue glass again—open. Blue glass away—shut. Blue glass again—open. Away—shut. Funny. Douglas experimented, trembling. Through the glass the eyes seemed to peer hungrily, avidly, through Mr. Koberman's closed lids. Without the blue glass they seemed tightly shut.

But it was the rest of Mr. Koberman's body . . .

Mr. Koberman's bedclothes dissolved off him. The blue glass had something to do with it. Or perhaps it was the clothes themselves, just being *on* Mr. Koberman. Douglas cried out.

He was looking through the wall of Mr. Koberman's stomach, right *inside* him!'

Mr. Koberman was solid.

Or, nearly so, anyway.

There were strange shapes and sizes within him.

Douglas must have stood amazed for five minutes, thinking about the blue worlds, the red worlds, the yellow worlds side by side, living together like glass panes around the big white stair window. Side by side, the colored panes, the different worlds, Mr. Koberman had said so himself.

So this was why the colored window had been broken.

"Mr. Koberman, wake up!"

No answer.

"Mr. Koberman, where do you work at night? Mr. Koberman, where do you work?"

A little breeze stirred the blue window shade.

"In a red world or a green world or a yellow one, Mr. Koberman?"

Over everything was a blue glass silence.

"Wait there," said Douglas.

He walked down to the kitchen, pulled open the great squeaking drawer and picked out the sharpest, biggest knife.

Very calmly he walked into the hall, climbed back up the stairs again, opened the door to Mr. Koberman's room, went in, and closed it, holding the sharp knife in one hand.

—

Grandma was busy fingering a piecrust into a pan when Douglas entered the kitchen to place something on the table.

"Grandma, what's this?"

She glanced up briefly, over her glasses. "I don't know."

It was square, like a box, and elastic. It was bright orange in color. It had four square tubes, colored blue, attached to it. It smelled funny.

"Ever see anything like it, Grandma?"

"No."

"That's what *I* thought."

Douglas left it there, went from the kitchen. Five minutes later he returned with something else. "How about *this?*"

He laid down a bright pink linked chain with a purple triangle at one end.

"Don't bother me," said Grandma. "It's only a chain."

Next time he returned with two hands full. A ring, a square, a triangle, a pyramid, a rectangle, and—other shapes. All of them were pliable, resilient, and looked as if they were made of gelatin. "This isn't all," said Douglas, putting them down. "There's more where this came from."

Grandma said, "Yes, yes," in a far-off tone, very busy.

"You were wrong, Grandma."

"About what?"

"About all people being the same inside."

"Stop talking nonsense."

"Where's my piggy bank?"

"On the mantel, where you left it."

"Thanks."

He tromped into the parlor, reached up for his piggy bank.

Grandpa came home from the office at five.

"Grandpa, come upstairs."

"Sure, son. Why?"

"Something to show you. It's not nice; but it's interesting."

Grandpa chuckled, following his grandson's feet up to Mr. Koberman's room.

"Grandma mustn't know about this; she wouldn't like it," said Douglas. He pushed the door wide open. "There."

Grandfather gasped.

Douglas remembered the next few hours all the rest of his life. Standing over Mr. Koberman's naked body, the coroner and his assistants. Grandma, downstairs, asking somebody, "What's going on up there?" and Grandpa saying, shakily, "I'll take Douglas away on a long vacation so he can forget this whole ghastly affair. Ghastly, ghastly affair!"

Douglas said, "Why should it be bad? I don't see anything bad. I don't feel bad."

The coroner shivered and said, "Koberman's dead, all right."

His assistant sweated. "Did you see those *things* in the pans of water and in the wrapping paper?"

"Oh, my God, my God, yes, I saw them."

"Christ."

The coroner bent over Mr. Koberman's body again. "This better be kept secret, boys. It wasn't murder. It was a mercy the boy acted. God knows what might have happened if he hadn't."

"What was Koberman? A vampire? A monster?"

"Maybe. I don't know. Something—not human." The coroner moved his hands deftly over the suture.

Douglas was proud of his work. He'd gone to much trouble. He had watched Grandmother carefully and remembered. Needle and thread and all. All in all, Mr. Koberman was as neat a job as any chicken ever popped into hell by Grandma.

"I heard the boy say that Koberman lived even after all those things were taken out of him." The coroner looked at the triangles and chains and pyramids floating in the pans of water. "Kept on *living*. God."

"Did the boy say that?"

"He did."

"Then, what *did* kill Koberman?"

The coroner drew a few strands of sewing thread from their bedding.

"This. . . ." he said.

Sunlight blinked coldly off a half-revealed treasure trove; six dollars and sixty cents' worth of silver dimes inside Mr. Koberman's chest.

"I think Douglas made a wise investment," said the coroner, sewing the flesh back up over the "dressing" quickly.

The Music on the Hill

By Saki

Sylvia Seltoun ate her breakfast in the morning room at Yessney with a pleasant sense of ultimate victory, such as a fervent Ironside might have permitted himself on the morrow of Worcester fight. She was scarcely pugnacious by temperament, but belonged to that more successful class of fighters who are pugnacious by circumstance. Fate had willed that her life should be occupied with a series of small struggles, usually with the odds slightly against her, and usually she had just managed to come through winning. And now she felt that she had brought her hardest and certainly her most important struggle to a successful issue. To have married Mortimer Seltoun, "Dead Mortimer" as his more intimate enemies called him, in the teeth of the cold hostility of his family, and in spite of his unaffected indifference to women, was indeed an achievement that had needed some determination and adroitness to carry through; yesterday she had brought her victory to its concluding stage by wrenching her husband away from Town and its group of satellite watering-places and "settling him down," in the vocabulary of her kind, in this remote wood-girt manor farm which was his country house.

"You will never get Mortimer to go," his mother had said carpingly, "but if he once goes he'll stay; Yessney throws almost as much a spell over him as Town does. One can understand what holds him to Town, but Yessney—" and the dowager had shrugged her shoulders.

There was a somber almost savage wildness about Yessney that was certainly not likely to appeal to town-bred tastes, and Sylvia, notwithstanding her name, was accustomed to nothing much more sylvan than "leafy Kensington." She looked on the country as something excellent and wholesome in its way, which was apt to become troublesome if you encouraged it overmuch. Distrust of townlife had been a new thing with her, born of her marriage with Mortimer, and she had watched with satisfaction the gradual fading of what she called "the Jermyn-Street-look" in his eyes as the woods and heather of Yessney had closed in on them yesternight. Her willpower and strategy had prevailed; Mortimer would stay. Outside the morning-room windows was a triangular slope of turf, which the indulgent might call a lawn, and beyond its low hedge of neglected fuchsia bushes a steeper slope of heather and bracken dropped down into cavernous combes overgrown with oak and yew. In its wild open savagery there seemed a stealthy linking of the joy of life with the terror of unseen things. Sylvia smiled complacently as she gazed with a School-of-Art appreciation at the landscape, and then of a sudden she almost shuddered.

—

"It is very wild," she said to Mortimer, who had joined her; "one could almost think that in such a place the worship of Pan had never quite died out."

"The worship of Pan never has died out," said Mortimer. "Other newer gods have drawn aside his votaries from time to time, but he is the Nature-God to whom all must come back at last. He has been called the Father of all the Gods, but most of his children have been stillborn."

Sylvia was religious in an honest, vaguely devotional kind of way, and did not like to hear her beliefs spoken of as mere aftergrowths, but it was at least something new and hopeful to hear Dead Mortimer speak with such energy and conviction on any subject.

"You don't really believe in Pan?" she asked incredulously.

"I've been a fool in most things," said Mortimer quietly, "but I'm not such a fool as not to believe in Pan when I'm down here. And if you're wise you won't disbelieve in him too boastfully while you're in his country."

It was not till a week later, when Sylvia had exhausted the attractions of the woodland walks round Yessney, that she ventured on a tour of inspection of the farm buildings. A farmyard suggested in her mind a scene of cheerful bustle, with churns and flails and smiling dairymaids, and teams of horses drinking knee-deep in duck-crowded ponds. As she wandered among the gaunt gray buildings of Yessney manor farm her first impression was one of crushing stillness and desolation, as though she had happened on some lone deserted homestead long given over to owls and cobwebs; then came a sense of furtive watchful hostility, the same shadow of unseen things that seemed to lurk in the wooded combes and coppices. From behind heavy doors and shuttered windows came the restless stamp of hoof or rasp of chain halter, and at times a muffled bellow from some stalled beast. From a distant comer a shaggy dog watched her with intent unfriendly eyes; as she drew near it slipped quietly into its kennel, and slipped out again as noiselessly when she had passed by. A few hens, questing for food under a rick, stole away under a gate at her approach. Sylvia felt that if she had come across any human beings in this wilderness of barn and byre they would have fled wraith-like from her gaze. At last, turning a corner quickly, she came upon a living thing that did not fly from her. Astretch in a pool of mud was an enormous sow, gigantic beyond the town-woman's wildest computation of swine-flesh, and speedily alert to resent and if necessary repel the unwonted intrusion. It was Sylvia's turn to make an unobtrusive retreat. As she threaded her way past rickyards and cowsheds and long blank walls, she started suddenly at a strange sound—the echo of a boy's laughter, golden and equivocal. Jan, the only boy employed on the farm, a tow-headed, wizen-faced yokel, was visibly at work on a potato clearing halfway up the nearest hillside, and Mortimer, when questioned, knew of no other probable or possible begetter of the hidden mockery that had ambushed Sylvia's retreat. The memory of that untraceable echo was added to her other impressions of a furtive sinister "something" that hung around Yessney.

Of Mortimer she saw very little; farm and woods and trout-streams seemed to swallow him up from dawn till dusk. Once, following the direction she had seen him take in the morning, she came to an open space in a nut copse, further shut in by huge yew trees, in the center of which stood a stone pedestal surmounted by a small bronze figure of a youthful Pan. It was a beautiful piece of workmanship, but her attention was chiefly held by the fact that a newly cut bunch of grapes had been placed as an offering at its feet. Grapes were none too plentiful at the manor house, and Sylvia snatched the bunch angrily from the pedestal. Contemptuous annoyance dominated her thoughts as she strolled slowly homeward, and then gave way to a sharp feeling of something that was very near fright; across a thick tangle of undergrowth a boy's face was scowling at her, brown and beautiful, with unutterably evil eyes. It was a lonely pathway, all pathways round Yessney were lonely for the matter of that, and she sped forward without waiting to give a closer scrutiny to this sudden apparition. It was not till she had reached the house that she discovered that she had dropped the bunch of grapes in her flight.

"I saw a youth in the wood today," she told Mortimer that evening, "brown-faced and rather handsome, but a scoundrel to look at. A gypsy lad, I suppose."

"A reasonable theory," said Mortimer, "only there aren't any gypsies in these parts at present."

"Then who was he?" asked Sylvia, and as Mortimer appeared to have no theory of his own she passed on to recount her finding of the votive offering.

"I suppose it was your doing," she observed; "it's a harmless piece of lunacy, but people would think you dreadfully silly if they knew of it."

"Did you meddle with it in any way?" asked Mortimer.

"I—I threw the grapes away. It seemed so silly," said Sylvia, watching Mortimer's impassive face for a sign of annoyance.

"I don't think you were wise to do that," he said reflectively. "I've heard it said that the Wood Gods are rather horrible to those who molest them."

"Horrible perhaps to those that believe in them, but you see I don't," retorted Sylvia.

"All the same," said Mortimer in his even, dispassionate tone, "I should avoid the woods and orchards if I were you, and give a wide berth to the horned beasts on the farm."

It was all nonsense, of course, but in that lonely wood-girt spot nonsense seemed able to rear a bastard brood of uneasiness.

"Mortimer," said Sylvia suddenly, "I think we will go back to Town some time soon."

Her victory had not been so complete as she had supposed; it had carried her on to ground that she was already anxious to quit.

"I don't think you will ever go back to Town," said Mortimer. He seemed to be paraphrasing his mother's prediction as to himself.

Sylvia noted with dissatisfaction and some self-contempt that the course of her next afternoon's ramble took her instinctively clear of the network of woods. As to the horned cattle, Mortimer's warning was scarcely needed, for she had always regarded them as of doubtful neutrality at the best: her imagination unsexed the most matronly dairy cows and turned them into bulls liable to "see red" at any moment. The ram who fed in the narrow paddock below the orchards she had adjudged, after ample and cautious probation, to be of docile temper; today, however, she decided to leave his docility untested, for the usually tranquil beast was roaming with every sign of restlessness from corner to corner of his meadow. A low, fitful piping, as of some reedy flute, was coming from the depth of a neighboring copse, and there seemed to be some subtle connection between the animal's restless pacing and the wild music from the wood. Sylvia turned her steps in an upward direction and climbed the heather-clad slopes that stretched in rolling shoulders high above Yessney. She had left the piping notes behind her, but across the wooded combes at her feet the wind brought her another kind of music, the straining bay of hounds in full chase. Yessney was just on the outskirts of the Devon-and-Somerset country, and the hunted deer sometimes came that way. Sylvia could presently see a dark body, breasting hill after hill, and sinking again and again out of sight as he crossed the combes, while behind him steadily swelled that relentless chorus, and she grew tense with the excited sympathy that one feels for any hunted thing in whose capture one is not directly interested. And at last he broke through the outermost line of oak scrub and fern and stood panting in the open, a fat September stag carrying a well-furnished head. His obvious course was to drop down to the brown pools of Undercombe, and thence make his way towards the red deer's favored sanctuary, the sea. To Sylvia's surprise, however, he turned his head to the upland slope and came lumbering resolutely onward over the heather. "It will be dreadful," she thought, "the hounds will pull him down under my very eyes." But the music of the pack seemed to have died away

A fat September stag carrying a well-furnished head.

for a moment, and in its place she heard again that wild piping, which rose now on this side, now on that, as though urging the failing stag to a final effort. Sylvia stood well aside from his path, half hidden in a thick growth of whortle bushes, and watched him swing stiffly upward, his flanks dark with sweat, the coarse hair on his neck showing light by contrast. The pipe music shrilled suddenly around her, seeming to come from the bushes at her very feet, and at the same moment the great beast slewed round and bore directly down upon her. In an instant her pity for the hunted animal was changed to wild terror at her own danger; the thick heather roots mocked her scrambling efforts at flight, and she looked frantically downward for a glimpse of oncoming hounds. The huge antler spikes were within a few yards of her, and in a flash of numbing fear she remembered Mortimer's warning, to beware of horned beasts on the farm. And then with a quick throb of joy she saw that she was not alone; a human figure stood a few paces aside, knee-deep in the whortle bushes.

—

"Drive it off!" she shrieked. But the figure made no answering movement.

The antlers drove straight at her breast, the acrid smell of the hunted animal was in her nostrils, but her eyes were filled with the horror of something she saw other than her oncoming death. And in her ears rang the echo of a boy's laughter, golden and equivocal.

The Boarded Window

By Ambrose Bierce

In 1830, only a few miles away from what is now the great city of Cincinnati, lay an immense and almost unbroken forest. The whole region was sparsely settled by people of the frontier—restless souls who no sooner had hewn fairly habitable homes out of the wilderness and attained to that degree of prosperity which today we should call indigence, then, impelled by some mysterious impulse of their nature, they abandoned all and pushed farther westward, to encounter new perils and privations in the effort to regain the meager comforts which they had voluntarily renounced. Many of them had already forsaken that region for the remoter settlements, but among those remaining was one who had been of those first arriving. He lived alone in a house of logs surrounded on all sides by the great forest, of whose gloom and silence he seemed a part, for no one had ever known him to smile nor speak a needless word. His simple wants were supplied by the sale or barter of skins of wild animals in the river town, for not a thing did he grow upon the land which, if needful, he might have claimed by right of undisturbed possession. There were evidences of "improvement"—a few acres of ground immediately about the house had once been cleared of its trees, the decayed stumps of which were half concealed by the new growth that had been suffered to repair the ravage wrought by the ax. Apparently the man's zeal for agriculture had burned with a failing flame, expiring in penitential ashes.

The little log house, with its chimney of sticks, its roof of warping clapboards weighted with traversing poles, and its "chinking" of clay, had a single door and, directly opposite, a window. The latter, however, was boarded up—nobody could remember a time when it was not. And none knew why it was so closed; certainly not because of the occupant's dislike of light and air, for on those rare occasions when a hunter had passed that lonely spot the recluse had commonly been seen sunning himself on his doorstep if heaven had provided sunshine for his need. I fancy there are few persons living today who ever knew the secret of that window, but I am one, as you shall see.

The man's name was said to be Murlock. He was apparently seventy years old, actually about fifty. Something besides years had had a hand in his aging. His hair and long, full beard were white, his gray, lusterless eyes sunken, his face singularly seamed with wrinkles which appeared to belong to two intersecting systems. In figure he was tall and spare, with a stoop of the shoulders—a burden bearer. I never saw him; these particulars I learned from my grandfather, from whom also I got the man's story when I was a lad. He had known him when living nearby in that early day.

One day Murlock was found in his cabin, dead. It was not a time and place for coroners and newspapers, and I suppose it was agreed that he had died from natural causes or I should have been told, and should remember. I know only that with what was probably a sense of the fitness of things the body was buried near the cabin, alongside the grave of his wife, who had preceded him by so many years that local tradition had retained hardly a hint of her existence. That closes the final chapter of this true story—excepting, indeed, the circumstance that many years afterward, in company with an equally intrepid spirit, I penetrated to the place and ventured near enough to the ruined cabin to throw a stone against it, and ran away to avoid the ghost which every well-informed boy thereabout knew haunted the spot. But there is an earlier chapter—that supplied by my grandfather.

When Murlock built his cabin and began laying sturdily about with his ax to hew out a farm—the rifle, meanwhile, his means of support—he was young, strong, and full of hope. In that eastern country whence he came he had married, as was the fashion, a young woman in all ways worthy of his honest devotion, who shared the dangers and privations of his lot with a willing spirit and light heart. There is no known record of her name; of her charms of mind and person tradition is silent and the doubter is at liberty to entertain his doubt; but God forbid that I should share it! Of their affection and happiness there is abundant assurance in every added day of the man's widowed life; for what but the magnetism of a blessed memory could have chained that venturesome spirit to a lot like that?

One day Murlock returned from gunning in a distant part of the forest to find his wife prostrate with fever, and delirious. There was no physician within miles, no neighbor; nor was she in a condition to be left, to summon help. So he set about the task of nursing her back to health, but at the end of the third day she fell into unconsciousness and so passed away, apparently, with never a gleam of returning reason.

From what we know of a nature like his we may venture to sketch in some of the details of the outline picture drawn by my grandfather. When convinced that she was dead, Murlock had sense enough to remember that the dead must be prepared for burial. In performance of this sacred duty he blundered now and again, did certain things incorrectly, and others which he did correctly were done over and over. His occasional failures to accomplish some simple and ordinary act filled him with astonishment, like that of a drunken man who wonders at the suspension of familiar natural laws. He was surprised, too, that he did not weep—surprised and a little ashamed; surely it is unkind not to weep for the dead. "Tomorrow," he said aloud, "I shall have to make the coffin and dig the grave; and then I shall miss her, when she is no longer in sight; but now—she is dead, of course, but it is all right—it *must* be all right, somehow. Things cannot be so bad as they seem."

He stood over the body in the fading light, adjusting the hair and putting the finishing touches to the simple toilet, doing all mechanically, with soulless care. And still through his consciousness ran an undersense of conviction that all was right—that he should have her again as before, and everything explained. He had had no experience in grief; his capacity had not been enlarged by use. His heart could not contain it all, nor his imagination rightly conceive it. He did not know he was so hard struck; *that* knowledge would come later, and never go. Grief is an artist of powers as various as the instruments upon which he plays his dirges for the dead, evoking from some the sharpest, shrillest notes, from others the low, grave chords that throb recurrent like the slow beating of a distant drum. Some natures it startles; some it stupefies. To one it comes like the stroke of an arrow, stinging all the sensibilities to a keener life; to another as the blow of a bludgeon, which in crushing benumbs. We may conceive Murlock to have been that way affected, for (and here we are upon surer ground than that of conjecture) no sooner had he finished his pious work than, sinking into a chair by the side of the table upon which the body lay, and noting how white the profile showed in the deepening gloom, he laid his arms upon the table's edge, and dropped his face into them, tearless yet and unutterably weary. At that moment came in through the open window a long, wailing sound like the cry of a lost child in the far deeps of the darkening wood! But the man did not move. Again, and nearer than before, sounded that unearthly cry upon his failing sense. Perhaps it was a wild beast; perhaps it was a dream. For Murlock was asleep.

Some hours later, as it afterward appeared, this unfaithful watcher awoke and lifting his head from his arms intently listened—he knew not why. There in the black darkness by the side of the dead, recalling all without a shock, he strained his eyes to see—he knew not what. His senses were all alert, his breath was suspended, his blood had stilled its tides as if to assist the silence. Who—what had waked him, and where was it?

Suddenly the table shook beneath his arms, and at the same moment he heard, or fancied that he heard, a light, soft step—another—sounds as of bare feet upon the floor!

He was terrified beyond the power to cry out or move. Perforce he waited—waited there in the darkness through seeming centuries of such dread as one may know, yet live to tell. He tried vainly to speak the dead woman's name, vainly to stretch forth his hand across the table to learn if she were there. His throat was powerless, his arms and hands were like lead. Then occurred something most frightful. Some heavy body seemed hurled against the table with an impetus that pushed it against his breast so sharply as nearly to overthrow him, and at the same instant he heard and felt the fall of something upon the floor with so violent a thump that the whole house was shaken by the impact. A scuffling ensued, and a confusion of sounds impossible to describe. Murlock had risen to his feet. Fear had by excess forfeited control of his faculties. He flung his hands upon the table. Nothing was there!

There is a point at which terror may turn to madness; and madness incites to action. With no definite intent, from no motive but the wayward impulse of a madman, Murlock sprang to the wall, with a little groping seized his loaded rifle, and without aim discharged it. By the flash which lit up the room with a vivid illumination, he saw an enormous panther dragging

He saw an enormous panther.

the dead woman toward the window, its teeth fixed in her throat! Then there were darkness blacker than before, and silence; and when he returned to consciousness the sun was high and the wood vocal with songs of birds.

The body lay near the window, where the beast had left it when frightened away by the flash and report of the rifle. The clothing was deranged, the long hair in disorder, the limbs lay anyhow. From the throat, dreadfully lacerated, had issued a pool of blood not yet entirely coagulated. The ribbon with which he had bound the wrists was broken; the hands were tightly clenched. Between the teeth was a fragment of the animal's ear.

Fingers on the Back of the Neck

By Margaret Mahy

When Ivor was very small and walking down the jetty with his great-grandmother, May, he liked to feel her fingers resting against the back of his neck. "Oops!" she would cry, catching him if he stumbled over the rough boards of the jetty deck. But by the time he was eight, interested in computer games and completely determined to go to St. Christopher's, the most stylish school in town, her affectionate touch irritated him. And by the time he was twelve, and her long fingers were so much more arthritic and knobbly, he could scarcely bear it.

"I hate the way she strokes my neck when we're out walking," he complained to his mother. "I hate the way she says 'Oops!' as if it was me who was almost falling over, not her."

"Put up with it," his mother said. "It'll all be worth it one day. She just adores you, and she's simply loaded." She meant that Great-Grandmother May was rich.

Rich! At first it had seemed a fair-tale word like "magician" or "unicorn." But, after a while, May's thick, pale carpets, her heavy silver spoons, and the pictures on her wall began whispering to Ivor, over and over again. "Rich! Rich! Rich!" said these voices every time he came to call. If, for some reason, his father couldn't afford the fees for St. Christopher's, Ivor believed May would help out. His mother always said she would. It came as a shock to find that May actually disapproved of private schools. She might be rich, but she had no sense of style, and Ivor's mother said style was everything.

Saturday after Saturday Ivor would take the bus over the hill, heading for the lonely edge of the harbor where Great-Grandmother May lived. And at some time, during every long, boring Saturday afternoon, May would suggest a walk down to the edge of the sea and along the jetty.

Sometimes, the tide was fully in and waves were breaking against the retaining wall. Sometimes, Ivor and May would find themselves staring out over a great expanse of shining mud, with the sea a mere slot of cloudy green in the distance. But, unlike the sea, the jetty did not change.

It was a long jetty and, as Ivor walked along it with May half a step behind him, he often felt that it was secretly stretching itself. Over all the weeks and months and years of Saturdays, he came to know it by heart. There was one thick plank with a twist in its cracked grain and a particular hollow knot hole that seemed to wink at him as he stepped over it. Another gave off a curiously resonant "clonk" whenever he stood on it, and then a softer, less definite sound when he moved off again. Seagulls and, occasionally, kingfishers, perching on the worm jetty railings, would watch Ivor and his great-grandmother strolling towards them, then fly off at the last moment. The seagulls circled lazily, often coming back to perch on the jetty rail once more, but the kingfishers shot away, like jewels exploding over the sea.

"Are you rich, May?" Ivor had once asked her when he was small.

"Oh, I've got enough put aside for a rainy day," she had answered rather disapprovingly, as if the word "rich" was a sort of swear word. So he hadn't liked to ask her just how much she had actually managed to save, and what would happen to all that money when she died.

Sometimes, he was allowed to put up a green tent in the scrambling garden and camp out all night. May did not camp with him, but she would sit at the door of the tent with a thermos of hot chocolate, which they shared as they listened to the snicker of possums, challenging one another among the branches of the plum tree, or the shuffle of summer hedgehogs. It was strange, however, that the enclosed and shadowy garden had none of the mystery that seemed to hang over the open, sunlit jetty. Or, perhaps, the mystery was not so much *around* it as actually *in* it, seeping invisibly out of all the cracks of age and weathering in its old wood.

And "Clonk"! The loose board always sounded its single note as he stepped on it, then sighed a little as he stepped off again. The rail always felt a little rough and splintery under his hand. And sooner or later, Great-Grandmother May, walking behind him rather more slowly than she had walked a few years earlier, would let her hand fall lightly and fondly on the back of Ivor's neck.

"The water's never quite clear . . . never *sparkling*," she once said. "But I've grown quite fond of this cloudy green. In a funny way it seems truer, because life's *cloudy*, don't you think?"

Ivor despised cloudy lives. He always thought of rich people as clear and sparkling. Rich people certainly preferred sparkling, sandy beaches, and, though his parents always seemed to be struggling to make enough money between them, they tried to live like rich people. Each Christmas they rented a holiday house beside a real ocean, where there was no harbor mouth to throttle big waves and surf. Swimming in this sea, Ivor felt sparkling, too. When these holidays were over and he and May walked along the jetty together, he would dream of that other sea, and of dry, white sand burning the soles of his feet.

"How did you get to be rich?" he asked his great-grandmother.

"I bought a piece of land some years ago," she said, "just before Meg died." (Meg was her daughter, Ivor's grandmother. She and her husband had been killed in a car accident before Ivor was born.) "And then I sold it for a lot of money. But, really, I'm well-to-do because I live simply . . . I don't spend a lot."

"Mum says you're rich," said Ivor. "She says you could help us a lot more than you do."

May was silent for a moment.

"You probably know that I think your parents *waste* money," she said at last. "And I don't like waste. I look after money carefully, because one of these days I'll probably have to pay someone to look after me." She broke off. She paused. "Oh, my goodness, what *has* happened here?"

An oval hole had been burned through the thick planks close to the jetty rail. It was still smoldering at the edges. Someone must have lit a fire on the jetty.

"Why would anyone do a stupid thing like that?" May said angrily. "Sheer vandalism!"

"It's burned right through," said Ivor. Peering into the blackened hole, he was fascinated to find the sea looking back at him. It was as if the jetty had suddenly grown an eye, black where human eyes were white, with a deep, shifty, green pupil. It was an eye with the power to read minds. He sprang back from the hole.

"I don't think it's dangerous," May said. "I mean, I don't think it's likely to start burning again. But I'll ring the Harbor Board when I get home."

They reached the end of the jetty. The tide was in and they walked down the steps to the very edge of the water.

"Be careful!" said May, as if he were still only a little kid of four. But Ivor barely heard her.

I looked into you, back there, the sea seemed to be telling him. *I saw what was in your heart.*

On their way home, he took care to walk as far as possible from the burned eye, and, by next Saturday, the hole was patched over with a square of tin. It gave out a clashing note of its own when Ivor stepped on it, which he often did, grinding his foot hard down, for, even though it was blinded, he knew the eye was still there under the lid, and that it always recognized his step.

By the time he turned twelve Ivor had mostly stopped visiting May, for, as he grew older, his parents began including him more and more in their own adventures.

"Let's *really* go away this Christmas," his mother said. "I don't just mean up north. Let's pop over to Oz . . . go to the Gold Coast. Have a wee gamble."

"Trust you to come up with a scheme like that," said his father, sounding both fond and irritated. "It hasn't been a great year, business-wise, and we'll have big school fees next year if Ivor goes to St. Christopher's."

"What do you mean—'if'?" asked Ivor, suddenly alarmed.

"Well, nothing's certain in this life," his father replied. "I do my best but I'm not *made* of money. And St. Christopher's—well, you know it's a very expensive school."

But Ivor's mother hooked her arm affectionately round his father's neck.

"All work and no play makes Jack a dull boy," she cried. "And Ivor and I don't like dull boys. We like cool Kit-cats." (Kit-cats were what the boys from St. Christopher's were often called.) "Anyhow, who knows? We might win enough to pay the fees ten times over."

"If I had a dollar for every time I've heard you come up with an argument like that, we'd be able to buy the whole school," said his father.

All the same they flew, business class, to the Gold Coast where the sea was sparkling and beautiful, and there was plenty of warm sand. The beaches were crowded, but Ivor loved crowds. He realized that the lonely old jetty had always frightened him in some way. It had always made him feel it was about to reveal some terrible accident. Yet nothing terrible had ever happened on the jetty. May would certainly have told him if it had. Of course May loved him—Ivor knew that—but he knew by now that he didn't particularly enjoy love, unless other good things went with it.

Halfway through the holiday, one of May's neighbors rang to tell them that May had had a bad fall. She was in a wheelchair, with neighbors watching over her, and a district nurse calling in once a day. "It was a bad break," the neighbor told Ivor's father. "When are you coming home?"

"In about five days," said Ivor's father. "We'd come sooner, but you know what the holiday season's like. Every flight is booked solid." When they did go back home, however, Ivor's father drove over to see May immediately. He came back, looking sad and troubled.

"She's not too bad," he said. "Well, she's frail, but reasonably cheerful. However . . ." He looked at Ivor and his mother cautiously. ". . . it might be a good idea for Ivor to forget about St. Kit's for a year or two." (Ivor and his mother cried out as if they had both been stabbed.) "No harm in going to a state school just for a bit, is there?"

"There's all the difference in the world," exclaimed Ivor's mother.

"Well, you should have thought of that before," Ivor's father snapped back. "I warned you over and over again. We spent a lot on that holiday, more than even I thought we'd spend. And May won't be able to help us."

"Why not?" cried Ivor's mother.

"She's going to need a full-time, live-in housekeeper to take care of her, and they don't come cheap," his father explained. "And she might live for years. Anyhow, I don't think she'd be too impressed if I asked her for money right now, even for Ivor. Not after our gambling holiday."

Ivor looked at his reflection in the looking glass over the sideboard. He looked strong and sure of himself . . . perfect Kit-cat material. While his parents argued behind him, he checked the paper for tide times. Fill tide was in the late afternoon.

The following day, Saturday, he took the bus as usual, delighted with himself for feeling so calm and business-like. This was what it was like to be grown up and in charge of life. All the same, it gave him a shock to see his great-grandmother so much thinner and frailer than she had looked even six weeks earlier. The flesh of her face draped over its bones, like a theater curtain, ready to drop and reveal the smiling skull below. May's eyes were more deeply sunken than they had been, her hair greasy and uncared-for. She looked up nervously as he came into the room, and then, when she saw it was Ivor, beamed with relief and pleasure.

"Ivor, my dear," she said. "What a lovely surprise! I didn't know you were coming."

"I just grabbed the chance," he said. "I've really missed you." He gave her a big bear-hug.

"Tea?" she asked him. Ivor glanced casually at his watch.

"Great!" he said. "But can we go for a walk first? Just to look at everything all over again."

"You go on your own," she said a little sadly. "You'll be freer without me."

"What? Go down the jetty without you?" cried Ivor. "No way!"

"I don't know how good this chair is on a rough road . . ." May sounded doubtful. "I have trouble using the brake, what with my arthritis. But why not?" she added bravely. "Nothing venture! Nothing win!"

"I'm strong," Ivor said, beaming. "And the wheelchair's got a seatbelt. I'll fasten you in."

The first part was easy, slightly downhill all the way along a nicely graded, main road. But then they turned on to the jetty road, with its potholes and corrugations, and the wheelchair grew harder to manage easily. May cried out in protest, half laughing and half alarmed.

"Oh, heavens, do be careful!"

"Don't worry," promised Ivor, leaning forward to touch the back of her neck as she had once touched his. "I'm going to take *very* good care of you."

"Bless you!" she said. She could not see the expression on his face as he spoke.

Having looked up the tide tables in the paper, Ivor knew exactly when the tide would be high. All the same it was a relief to him when they came round the corner to see spray splashing up above the sea wall. The water would be deep at the far end of the jetty.

"It *is* lovely to see this view again," May said. "I'm glad you made me come. Now, let's go along the jetty, and then hurry back home because I'm beginning to feel rather cold."

"Poor May," said Ivor teasingly. Perhaps he had overdone it, for she suddenly twisted round, trying to look back at him as well as she could.

"Here we go!" he cried heartily, and ran down on to the jetty, pushing her in front of him.

"Stop, Ivor! Stop!" she called breathlessly, but he did not stop. They jolted and swayed along the jetty. "Clonk," went one particular board under his feet, but there were many loose boards these days. "Twang!" went the tin lid, still lowered over the burned eye. May was silent as her knobbly fingers struggled desperately first with the brake, and then with the catch on the seatbelt. Out beyond the harbor mouth the evening was clear, the sky the color of pure honey. Ivor raced the whole length of the jetty, gathering speed towards the end, even though his lungs were bursting, and then, with a final, violent thrust, he sent the wheelchair hurtling down the steps and into the sea. Carried by its own weight and momentum, it toppled straight into the water.

"Oops!" Ivor cried, and actually mimed concern even though he was quite alone. Only now did he truly realize how frightened he had been that May might free herself. If she had bobbed to the surface, he would have had to hold her under, and that would have been horrible. But the chair sank rapidly, taking May with it. He thought he heard her say his name once. Then the water closed over her head and she was gone.

In the end the water grew calm again. The muddy discoloration which had risen to the surface began to dissipate. And at last Ivor felt free . . . free to turn, free to scream as he ran back along the jetty, loose boards drumming urgently under his feet. If his first screams were odd, mechanical cries, by the time his rubber sandals thudded down on the tin lid of the eye, he was screaming in good earnest. Real tears were pouring down his face. There was no one to hear, just as there had been no one to see him. Once on the main road he ran towards the general store, waving desperately at every passing car. The first two drove on, but the third stopped, and he was able to sob out his dreadful tale. His great-grandmother had insisted he take her for a walk, even though he wasn't used to the chair. He had been turning the wheelchair at the end of the jetty, and somehow its front wheel had gone over the top step, and somehow . . . somehow . . .

Ivor wept. It was something he could do quite easily. He wept at intervals for the rest of the evening, while people told him it was not his fault . . . that it had been a terrible accident. As Ivor repeated his story over and over again, he began to believe it himself. It seemed as if it must be true. And then an odd thing happened. As he wept for the last time that evening, his hands across his streaming eyes, he suddenly saw with great clarity a vision no bigger than a bright postage stamp. There was the jetty, dark against the green water. There was its reflection in the sea below, and there, leaning on the railing, was someone holding a bunch of white and yellow flowers. The shock of this sudden picture made Ivor gasp.

"Darling," said his mother. "Poor boy!" He took his hands from his face, and looked at her out of swollen eyes. "What a nightmare!" she went on. "But listen, Ivor, I know it seems a callous thing to say, but it wouldn't have been much fun for her from now on. It would have been downhill all the way. It's for the best . . . really, it's for the best." And then she gave him the look of someone sharing a terrible secret, which was almost as alarming as the vision of the figure with the flowers.

After the funeral, Ivor and his parents, along with a few close friends, took a short memorial walk down the jetty. Ivor's father had a fancy to throw flowers into the sea at the spot where May had so often stood gazing up at the sky or out to the mouth of the harbor.

"*You* carry them, Ivor," said his father. "She'd like *you* to be the one to throw them into the sea for her."

Ivor could not refuse. He took the flowers, hiding his horror. They were not from a florist. This posy had been gathered from May's own garden—yellow and white daisies mixed with yellow and white roses. Walking down the jetty behind his father, his palms pressed against the stems, Ivor felt those stems changing. Suddenly, they felt exactly like May's knobbly fingers. They shifted against his palm, then curled around his own hand and gave it a gentle squeeze.

"Now!" said his father, and Ivor threw the flowers into the water at the exact spot where the wheelchair had sunk four days earlier, shuddering as he did so. The flowers bobbed gently on the slow, green ripples.

I-vor! *I*-vor! *I*-vor! said the loose boards in rattling voices, as sober black shoes walked over them. Though Ivor edged as far away as possible from the tin patch, he knew the eye beneath it was watching him.

"She loved this old jetty," his father said.

"Yes," Ivor's mother agreed, "and you know, it is quite beautiful here. Wouldn't she love to think of us using the house for weekends?"

"Oh, no! It'll be too sad, without May," said Ivor quickly. Several friends glanced at him approvingly.

It was a great relief when it was all over, and they were back in the city again.

"Well, at least you will be able to go to St. Kit's," said his father. "If you're sure you want to, that is."

"I am sure," said Ivor, surprised at his own calm voice. "I want it more than anything."

In due course he went to St. Christopher's, and, though he did not forget the harbor and the jetty, or the wheelchair sinking slowly but steadily from sight, it seemed a small price to pay for the life he now had. Both his parents seemed so relieved and happy, and he had the pleasure of being one of the Kit-cats . . . the top cats in town. Occasionally, some people looked critically at his school uniform, but these were triumphant moments, for Ivor knew that they were all secretly jealous of him.

But then, one day, as he put his hand on the railing in the sports pavilion, he felt, not the smooth paint, but the familiar cracked and splintering wood of the jetty rail. There was no doubt about it. At the same time, the breeze, blowing across the sports ground, suddenly filled with the familiar scent of mud and salt, and of seaweed drying, even rotting a little, at an invisible high-tide line. "Clonk," said a loose board under his foot, and he thought his heart would stop with sheer fright.

And once these illusions had begun, they happened more and more frequently. The corridors at school stretched themselves before him rather as the jetty had once stretched itself, seeming to promise a dark surprise somewhere along the way. Ivor walked steadily on, hoping the illusion would disappear. It did, only to come again the next day . . . and the day after that, as well.

At the end of the week, angry and frightened, he decided to take the bus over the hill, one last time. By walking down the jetty on a bright day, he meant to remind himself that it was merely an old, wooden jetty, slowly falling to pieces. This might stop its ghostly intrusions into his city life. The jetty belonged to the *sea* side of the hill, and must not be allowed to invade his city side as well.

The bus stopped and he got out, walking quickly past May's old house which now wore a desolate, overgrown air. Down the familiar, winding road he walked, and around the corner. A film of water lying across the mud reflected the blue sky and the hills so perfectly it filled him with amazement. It was as if he were seeing two separate worlds, set edge to edge. Yet the reflected world was not a perfect duplication of the real one. It was a little smudged as if he were seeing it through a faint haze . . . a faint fog. Quickly! thought Ivor. Down the jetty—for the last time ever, with a bit of luck. Don't hurry! Don't seem scared in any way! After all, there's nothing to be afraid of. It's all in the mind.

As he stepped on to the jetty, he felt a curious shock. The whole world seemed to flick out of existence for a second and then flick back again. Ivor paused as he looked around. Sky, hills, jetty . . . everything was in place. But that haze was not just a haze but a real fog . . . and how it surged to meet him as he took a step towards it! Where had *that* come from so quickly? Within a moment it was all around him. But Ivor had walked along the jetty on other foggy days. He knew he could not possibly get lost. "Clonk," sang the loose board under his foot, then it sighed a little as he stepped off it again. Other loose boards began rattling a chant of *I*-vor! *I*-vor! *I*-vor! The fog was so thick by now that it was no longer possible to see ahead. So he watched his moving feet and suddenly, there was the burned eye watching him go by. Someone had prized the tin lid away. Funny, thought Ivor, pausing. He frowned. Hadn't the tide been out? Yet the sea was definitely surging on the other side of that blackened hole. And listen! There! And there again! He could hear the chuckle and slap of waves against the jetty piles.

The fog shifted and parted a little. The tide was indeed fully in, rippling closely under the deck of the jetty. Something bobbed on the ripples . . . a bunch of white and yellow flowers . . . daisies and roses as fresh as the day he had thrown them into the water all those months ago.

Suddenly, Ivor knew he could go no further. He would just have to put up with the ghosts on the other side of the hill. And if he were calm and

Where had that come from so quickly?

brave he would probably grow out of them. Anything—*anything*—was better than this. Turning, he began to walk briskly through the fog, back down the jetty again.

"Clonk," sang a board under his foot. He stopped short. It had sounded too soon. It had sounded . . . Ivor shook his head as if he were flicking something unpleasant out of his ears and walked on. And there was the eye, watching him retreat. *I*-vor! *I*-vor! *I*-vor! said the rattling chorus under his feet. Only a few more yards now, and he'd be on land again. It was at this moment Ivor became certain that someone was walking behind him. He couldn't quite say how he knew, for his own footsteps were the only ones he could hear. All the same, he knew the fog was inhabited. Straining his ears to hear the least sound, he scarcely noticed when he passed the burned eye a second and then a third time. But, when he saw it for the fourth time, he understood. He had stepped out of the real world, and was now walking through another, terrible place.

Back in the real world, he was suddenly sure, the sun was shining on an old jetty. Back in the *real* world, that old jetty was standing up to its ankles in mud and water and the tide was out. But he was doomed to walk endlessly in either direction, for *this* jetty would go on forever into infinite fog. "Clonk!" Yes, of course! He would hear that sound over and over and over again. And there was the eye, watching him go by once more. It would watch him forever. And those white and yellow flowers would always be bobbing along beside him.

Whatever the thing was in the fog behind him, it was definitely moving closer and closer. Ivor strode on, like a true St. Christopher boy, because he *had* to. If he hesitated, even for a second, he would fall. He tried to keep ahead. At last he even tried to run, but his foot caught on an uneven board and he stumbled.

"Oops!" said a voice behind him—a voice as soft as a small ripple flopping gently on mud. Knobbly fingers stroked the back of his neck, lightly and lovingly, and Ivor knew that this time their soft caress would last forever.

The Cremation of Sam McGee

By Robert W. Service

THERE ARE strange things done in the midnight sun
 By the men who moil for gold;
The Arctic trails have their secret tales
 That would make your blood run cold;
The Northern Lights have seen queer sights,
 But the queerest they ever did see
Was that night on the marge of Lake Lebarge
 I cremated Sam McGee.

Now Sam McGee was from Tennessee,
 where the cotton blooms and blows.
Why he left his home in the South to roam
 'round the Pole, God only knows.
He was always cold, but the land of gold
 seemed to hold him like a spell;
Though he'd often say in his homely way
 that he'd sooner live in Hell.

On a Christmas Day we were mushing our way
 over the Dawson trail.
Talk of your cold! through the parka's fold
 it stabbed like a driven nail.

If our eyes we'd close, then the lashes froze
    till sometimes we couldn't see;
It wasn't much fun, but the only one
    to whimper was Sam McGee.

And that very night, as we lay packed tight
    in our robes beneath the snow,
And the dogs were fed, and the stars o'erhead
    were dancing heel and toe,
He turned to me, and "Cap," says he,
    "I'll cash in this trip, I guess;
And if I do, I'm asking that you
    won't refuse my last request."

Well, he seemed so low that I couldn't say no;
    then he says with a sort of moan,
"It's the cursed cold, and it's got right hold
    till I'm chilled clean through to the bone.
Yet 'tain't being dead—it's my awful dread
    of the icy grave that pains;
So I want you to swear that, foul or fair,
    you'll cremate my last remains."

A pal's last need is a thing to heed,
    so I swore I would not fail;
And we started on at the streak of dawn;
    but God! he looked ghastly pale.
He crouched on the sleigh, and he raved all day
    of his home in Tennessee;
And before nightfall a corpse was all
    that was left of Sam McGee.

There wasn't a breath in that land of death,
    and I hurried, horror-driven,

With a corpse half hid that I couldn't get rid,
because of a promise given;
It was lashed to the sleigh, and it seemed to say,
"You may tax your brawn and brains,
But you promised true, and it's up to you
to cremate those last remains."

Now a promise made is a debt unpaid,
and the trail has its own stern code.
In the days to come, though my lips were dumb,
in my heart how I cursed that load.
In the long, long night, by the lone firelight,
while the huskies, round in a ring,
Howled out their woes to the homeless snow—
O God! how I loathed the thing.

And every day that quiet clay
seemed to heavy and heavier grow;
And on I went, though the dogs were spent
and the grub was getting low;
The trail was bad, and I felt half mad,
but I swore I would not give in;
And I'd often sing to the hateful thing,
and it hearkened with a grin.

Till I came to the marge of Lake Lebarge,
and a derelict there lay;
It was jammed in the ice, but I saw in a trice
it was called the Alice May.
And I looked at it, and I thought a bit,
and I looked at my frozen chum;
Then "Here," said I, with a sudden cry,
"is my cre-ma-tor-eum!"

Some planks I tore from the cabin floor,
and I lit the boiler fire;
Some coal I found that was lying around,
and I heaped the fuel higher;
The flames just soared, and the furnace roared
such a blaze you seldom see;
And I burrowed a hole in the glowing coal,
and I stuffed in Sam McGee.

Then I made a hike, for I didn't like
to hear him sizzle so;
And the heavens scowled, and the huskies howled,
and the wind began to blow.
It was icy cold, but the hot sweat rolled
down my cheeks, and I don't know why;
And the greasy smoke in an inky cloak
went streaking down the sky.

I do not know how long in the snow
I wrestled with grisly fear;
But the stars came out and they danced about
ere again I ventured near;
I was sick with dread, but I bravely said,
"I'll just take a peep inside.
I guess he's cooked, and it's time I looked."
Then the door I opened wide.

And there sat Sam, looking cool and calm,
in the heart of the furnace roar;
And he wore a smile you could see a mile,
and he said: "Please close that door.
It's fine in here, but I greatly fear
you'll let in the cold and storm—
Since I left Plumtree, down in Tennessee,
it's the first time I've been warm."

"It's the first time I've been warm."

There are strange things done in the midnight sun
    By the men who moil for gold;
The Arctic trails have their secret tales
    That would make your blood run cold;
The Northern Lights have seen queer sights,
    But the queerest they ever did see
Was that night on the marge of Lake Lebarge
    I cremated Sam McGee.

CREDITS

SPECIAL THANKS TO Cheryl Blanchard and Alice Wand, librarians at the Paine Memorial Free Library in Willsboro, New York, for their help in searching for many more stories than could be included in this volume. Thanks also to Marian Reiner for her invaluable assistance in clearing the permissions.

Permission to reprint the following works is gratefully acknowledged:

"The Man Upstairs" by Ray Bradbury. Copyright © 1947 by *Harper's Magazine*, renewed 1974 by Minneapolis Star & Tribune Co. Reprinted by permission of Don Congdon Associates, Inc.

"The Lottery" from *The Lottery and Other Stories* by Shirley Jackson. Copyright © 1948, 1949 by Shirley Jackson. Copyright renewed 1976, 1977 by Laurence Hyman, Barry Hyman, Mrs. Sarah Webster, and Mrs. Joanne Schnurer. Reprinted by permission of Farrar, Straus and Giroux, LLC.

"Here There Be Tygers" from *Skeleton Crew* by Stephen King. Copyright © Stephen King. Reprinted with permission. All rights reserved.

"Thanksgiving" from *Haunted: Tales of the Grotesque* by Joyce Carol Oates. Copyright © 1994 by *The Ontario Review, Inc.* Used by permission of Dutton, a division of Penguin Group (USA) Inc.

"Miriam" from *The Complete Collected Stories of Truman Capote* by Truman Capote. Copyright © 2004 by The Truman Capote Literary Trust. Used by permission of Random House, Inc.

"Genesis and Catastrophe" from *The Best of Roald Dahl* by Roald Dahl. Copyright © 1990 by Roald Dahl. Used by permission of Vintage Books, a division of Random House, Inc.

"Kittens" from *Strange Highways* by Dean Koontz. Copyright © 1995 by Dean Koontz. Used by permission of Warner Books, Inc.

"Fingers on the Back of the Neck" by Margaret Mahy. Copyright © 1996 by Margaret Mahy. Reprinted by permission of Lemniscaat Publishers and Watson, Little, Ltd. as licensing agents.